HONEYMOON

Fr. Richard A. Infante

HONEYMOON

And Other Pilgrimage Stories

Richard Infante

LAMBING
PRESS

Contents

Foreword

by Mike Aquilina

Some years back I committed an essay in which I asserted that the "road story" was the archetypal American tale. For evidence I cited Mark Twain's Huckleberry Finn and Jack Kerouac's collected works, Whitman's "Song of the Open Road," and even Bob Hope and Bing Crosby's twenty-year movie franchise. I made no argument, really, as I thought the citations made the case.

The ink had hardly dried on my essay when I got a call from a dear friend and frequent foil. He wanted to know how I could make such a claim while apparently sober. I assured him that I could pass a blood test, and I stood by my thesis and its brief peripatetic bibliography.

He was having none of it. Had I never heard of Geoffrey Chaucer? Did I think Chaucer was American? What about Cervantes? Or turn the calendar back a couple thousand years: How about Homer's Odyssey? The Acts of the Apostles? Lucian's Peregrinus? Egeria's pilgrim diary? Remember the medieval quests for the

Holy Grail? Dante's Divine Comedy? I cried uncle. As he ranted the titles, my mind began to supply others.

A road trip, my friend concluded, was just a great way to tell a story. It came with a suitcase full of gimmicks for keeping reader interest. You can change the scenery: climb a mountain, ford a stream. You can introduce new characters-and dismiss them when they're no longer useful. No need to kill them. Just pack up and move on to the next town.

There's nothing particularly American about literary wandering. Nor is there anything peculiarly Christian about it. Lucian's Peregrinus is an anti-Christian satire! The road trip is deeply American, my friend concluded, only because it's deeply human.

OK. OK. But there is something more to the trip than the author's convenience. In real life, so many of our trips have religious significance. We see them within a story much larger than our annual break from work— and even larger than our lives. Pilgrim tourism is an industry that trades tens of billions of dollars every year through more than a hundred million pilgrimages—to Compostela, Mecca, Jerusalem, Rome, Montreal, Guadalupe.

Such voyages may come just once in an individual's life, but they give shape and meaning to smaller ventures: our Sunday drive to church, the yearly trek to visit our in-laws for Christmas, the miles we travel for funerals and weddings. Our conversations and our thoughts track the scenery as it changes. Memory really is a lane.

We discover that our itinerary is longer than we thought, and every stop changes us. We are moving Godward, and we see ourselves in his changing light. It's not that he changes. It's that the light reaches us differently depending on where we stand. The light looks different in Rio than it does in Wilmerding, and so do we.

Both G.K. Chesterton and T.S. Eliot made the same observation. We walk round the whole world till we get home, so that we can know home—and ourselves—for the first time.

It's God himself who taught us to do this, by making the voyage from heaven to earth and then back again, all for our sake.

In these pages, Richard Infante does something deeply human, deeply Christian, deeply American. In fact, he does something deeply divine. He guides us on other people's journeys of discovery, and he makes them ours, all for our sake.

Vessel of Life

"It still hurts, Mom," Katie whispered, leaning closer to her mother, whose arm was around the girl's shoulder.

"I know, dear," Mrs. Bradley said and softly stroked her blond hair. "The cramps should ease some by the time we get home."

They had been on the bus ride back to Lancaster for a couple of hours already. Katie's cramps were still severe, the second Tylenol only beginning to have an effect since they left Washington, D.C.

"How's she doing?" Mr. Bradley turned around and whispered to his wife.

"She'll be alright," Janet tried to reassure the both of them. "She'll sleep when we get home."

The bus swerved on the wet interstate highway, causing Katie to press closer to her mother.

"Is she still sick?" little Jesse said as he leaned over the back of his seat.

"Turn around," William directed his son. "Leave them be."

The temperature in the bus was, at times, too warm for Katie, so she had pulled her arms out of the sleeves of her blue winter coat and draped it loosely around her like a blanket. The bus from Our Lady of Lourdes Parish was nearly full, causing the air to seem stale and odorous to Katie. No matter how she squirmed in her seat, she could not get quite comfortable.

Janet and William had taken their family to the March for Life on the parish bus for the past few years. This year, with Holly away at the University of Maryland, they had planned to meet her at the March with her college's Respect Life Group, but things did not work out the way that they had hoped. Shortly after they had arrived at the National Basilica of the Immaculate Conception, Katie was beset with her first menstruation and Janet had to take her to the Ladies' Room in the crypt downstairs to help her manage. Meanwhile, William and Jesse had stayed in the narthex of the beautiful basilica praying the rosary with hundreds of other pilgrims who had come from various states in defense of the unborn. When the rosary was completed, they had walked around the enormous church visiting some of the shrines dedicated to the many devotional titles or apparitions of the Blessed Virgin Mary. Eventually, William and Jesse had gone downstairs in the hope that Katie and Janet would be ready to join them on the March. But when they saw them, they were huddled on a bench outside of the Ladies' Room, Janet wiping her daughter's face with tissues.

"I don't think we can go," Janet had said to William. "I gave her something for the pain, but she can't be jostled in the cold with that crowd."

"Do you want us to stay?" William had asked his wife.

"No, no. We'll be fine here," Janet had said. "You and Jesse go on the March. Here's the tickets for the subway," she had said and took the tickets out of her purse. "Don't forget to look for Holly's group with their big red banner. Just have the bus pick us up when the March is over. There's a noon Mass upstairs."

But by the time William and Jesse left the Basilica and took the train to join the marchers, the speakers had finished addressing the rally on the ellipse and the first wave of people had already marched the length of Constitution Avenue. Holly's college group of forty, or so, had been among the first to arrive at the formidable steps of the Supreme Court building, holding a large red banner with their university's name. Meanwhile, William and Jesse had just started their trek up the wide avenue teeming with tens of thousands of demonstrators, intermittently chanting: "Life yes; abortion no. Roe v. Wade has got to go." When they finally reached the court building, Holly and her young colleagues had already left for their appointment with a sympathetic congressman at the Capitol building.

It was about three-thirty when William and Jesse returned to the Basilica to get Janet and Katie. As they

3

boarded their bus, William explained to Janet that they had missed Holly's group at the steps of the court. In the late afternoon, the traffic in D.C. was heavy; it took them more than an hour just to get out of the city.

Janet had been tending Katie for the past few hours. The teenager was relieved to be on the bus heading home, but the ride was a little rough and aggravated her discomfort. Her mother had been a great help, but all she wantedto do was crawl into her bed and sleep the pain away. Despite her drowsiness, she overheard her father and brother talking about the day's excursion.

"That was the first time a president addressed the March in person," Mr. Bradley explained to Jesse. "Even though we got there too late to hear him, it was an historic moment for the pro-life movement."

"I remember seeing his video message on the big screen last year," Jesse said.

"That's what makes this year so special," William said. "The president came out himself to encourage the marchers."

Their brief dialogue caused Katie to turn in her seat and try to cover her head with the collar of her coat. Janet helped her arrange it around her neck and over her ears.

The bus slowed down as it took the exit. Fr. Powell announced on the microphone that they were making a brief stop for convenience and food. The lights were turned on above the aisle.

"We're in Pennsylvania, Jess," Mr. Bradley said as they got out of their seats with the other passengers. He stooped to pick up one of his gloves that had fallen out of his coat pocket. "We'll be in Lancaster pretty soon."

Janet waved them away as she and Katie decided to stay on the bus. "Get us a couple of those waters in the compartment above," she said to her husband.

"Here, honey," William said as he gave her the bottles of water. "Do you want me to get you something to eat?"

"Maybe a bag of potato chips," Janet said. "Plain ones, not flavored."

There was a little commotion as the pilgrims filed by them in the aisle, but most just let the women alone.

With the parked bus mostly empty except for a few others, Katie felt comfortable enough to talk with her mother about the day's ordeal.

"When did you first get your period, Mom?" she asked.

"About the same age as you—thirteen," Mrs. Bradley said. "Every woman has to go through it—some start younger, some older."

"It's not fair," Katie said. "Boys don't have to go through it."

"It's the price we pay for being vessels of life," Janet said. "It's a necessary part of God's design for making us the bearers of babies that grow within our bodies. It's mysterious and beautiful at the same time." "Then why do they want to kill them?" Katie asked.

"I don't think most really do," her mother said. "They're afraid of caring for the child. They've forgotten who they are—endowed with this gift of bringing life into the world."

"How come they can't see it?" Katie's blue eyes winced with a sharp cramp.

"They've forgotten that God has made us this way for a purpose," Janet explained to her daughter. "The day you were born was one of the happiest days of my life because the good Lord had given us another beautiful baby girl that I had carried for nine months."

"What about Jesse?" Katie managed a mischievous smile with the question.

"Him, too," Janet smiled. "Though sometimes I have my doubts." They tried to suppress their laughter but they were giggling aloud, even though it caused Katie some discomfort.

"Do you mind if we sit up here with you until my husband gets back?" the young dark-haired mother said, cradling her baby boy who awakened in her arms. "I'm Lisa and this is Jonathan; my husband is Frank."

"Please," Mrs. Bradley said. "I'm Janet and this is my daughter, Katie. How old is he?"

"He's almost two," Lisa said. "We weren't going to bring him, but he's better than a banner and the weather wasn't too bad."

"He's a cutie," Janet said and waved her fingers at the baby boy across the aisle nestled in his mother's arms. Jonathan smiled at her gesture.

Katie looked at the beautiful baby intently, understanding that he was what all the fuss was about: pregnancy, abortion, the March, the experience of her initial period.

"Were you the ones with the baby stroller?" Katie asked.

"Yes," Lisa said. "I bundled him up like an Eskimo; thank God it wasn't too cold."

Janet and Lisa chatted for a few minutes; all the while Katie gazed at the smiling baby boy secure in his young mother's embrace. Eventually, Janet reached across the aisle and held Jonathan's tiny fingers. He made a kind of gurgling laughter in response to her touch.

When the parishioners started to return, Lisa said her goodbyes and waved Jonathan's little arm at the ladies as she returned to their seats near the back of the bus.

William handed Janet the bag of potato chips, the brand she preferred. "We had hamburgers and french fries," he said. "Pretty good." He was relieved that Janet took care of Katie throughout the day as he wasn't prepared to help her in her delicate condition. As the bus pulled out onto the interstate, again, William overheard their secretive feminine whispers, which sounded like a foreign language to him, a language in which he would never be quite fluent.

The bus was dark, again, and most of the pilgrims tried to sleep or talked quietly following their day's demonstration. They had prayed the rosary together when they first left the capital and now were thankful for a little peace and quiet. The dark bus felt almost like a cocoon sheltering the pilgrims from the cold January rains that had started ever since they left Washington.

The final leg of the ride home would be comfortable enough for most of the passengers. Because their parish had been going on the March for about a decade, the committee knew to order a new motor coach months ahead with headrests, wider seats and leg room. The Bradley family had been going the past few years, ever since Jesse had turned seven years old; old enough, they figured, to understand why they were marching and strong enough to endure the crowded walk through the nation's capital. Younger families than theirs were evident throughout the March the past few years.

Janet and Katie shared the potato chips and sipped their tepid waters. "Mom, are we going to take the Nativity set down tomorrow?" Katie asked as her cramps eased some.

"Yes we are," Mrs. Bradley said. "We've kept it on the mantle the last few years until we came back from the March. It reminds us that Jesus came into the world as a vulnerable baby, too."

"I love the figurines of baby Jesus, Mary and Joseph," Katie said. They're so detailed and colorful."

"We got them when we were first married," Janet said. "It helps us remember that every human life is sacred in God's eyes. That's why our family goes on the March." Janet took the bottle of water from Katie's hand when she noticed her eyes drooping. She was thankful that her daughter could settle into a light sleep with her pain subsiding.

Revived with the food and drink, William and Jesse continued to discuss the day's adventure.

"What was the name of that big church again, Dad?" Jesse asked his father.

"The National Basilica of the Immaculate Conception," William answered. "The Blessed Mother is the patroness of our country under the title of the Immaculate Conception."

"That means that she gave birth to Jesus, right?" Jesse said.

"Not exactly," William corrected his son. "It means that the Blessed Virgin Mary was conceived without original sin so that she could bear the sinless Son of God."

"Hunh?" Jesse said, still a little confused.

"Don't you remember the story Fr. Powell told at the altar server Christmas party?" William asked. "That's the name Mary called herself when she appeared to little Bernadette at Lourdes."

"I kinda remember," Jesse defended his lapsed memory.

With Katie finally resting comfortably, Janet closed her eyes, trying to decompress from the day's ordeal. While the bus rumbled down the highway, she found a few minutes to calm her maternal anxiety over her daughter's threshold change on this day of all days. Her thoughts drifted through the morning's trauma at the Basilica, the intimate feminine care she provided her daughter, and the strained hours of waiting for the bus ride home. Katie had bravely endured the day's challenges and Janet was grateful that she had been with her as her girl's body continued its transformation into a woman's. Still and quiet in the dark bus, Janet overheard some of the conversation between the women sitting across the aisle from them.

"What's it called?" the younger woman asked her friend. "Microchimerism," the other woman said. "Dr. Walters has us doing some tests in the lab and it's amazing. The cells of the fetus pass through the placenta, into the mother's circulatory system and then adhere to some of her tissue, integrating into her organs like the brain, the breast, and the bone marrow."

"I knew that the mother's cells were part of the developing baby in the womb," her friend said. "But I didn't realize that it worked the other way, too."

"It's amazing," the technician said. "No wonder we feel so close to our kids—we're carrying their cells in our body like they have ours."

While she didn't quite understand the physiology of it all, Janet heard enough to realize that the bond with her daughters and son was even deeper than she had thought, reaching into the very cells of her maternal body. But it made sense to her on some instinctual level, helping to explain the intimate intuitions that she experienced with her children, almost as if she could feel what they felt, her maternal anxieties rooted in the profound union she shared with them.

"How is she doing?" Fr. Powell stopped to ask Janet as he walked up the aisle checking on his parishioners.

"She's a little better, now," Janet said to her kind priest and gently patted Katie's shoulder as she slept with her head resting against the cool window of the bus.

"She'll never forget this trip," the young priest said as he continued up the aisle.

"Neither will I," Janet said under her breath. For all the marches in Washington that she had attended with her family, for all her work with the parish's Respect Life Group, for the innumerable prayers that she had offered for the souls of the unborn, this was the pilgrimage that would leave an indelible mark in her maternal memory because it was not so much about the issue of abortion but more so about her beloved daughter and the mystery of life as ordained by God.

Within several minutes, the bus turned into the large parking lot of Our Lady of Lourdes Parish where they had left their cars.

"Jan, you better wake her up," William said as he rose from his seat. "We're home."

Mason-Dixon Line

Mr. Carnivali had just finished looking over the third quarter progress reports of the eighth grade students in his school, glad to see that no one was failing, even Bobby Murray. He was waiting for Mr. Weber, his eighth grade homeroom and upper grade social studies teacher to stop in the office during his mid-morning break. While he waited, he picked up the mahogany and brass nameplate on his desk, which he had received from the faculty for his twenty-fifth anniversary a few years ago, with the matching pen and pencil holder, and a sleek letter opener. Tools of the trade, he thought.

He probably wants to discuss the graduation ceremony for next month, or maybe next week's field trip, he speculated. Mr. Weber was one of the best and most popular teachers at Saint Thomas Aquinas Catholic School. Mr. Carnivali was happy when the young man had volunteered to take over the eighth grade field trip a few years ago, freeing him from the all-day pilgrimage to Emmitsburg and Gettysburg. After nearly twenty years, Peter Carnivali knew the trip backwards and forwards, but was more than glad to relinquish the duty to a younger man, especially now that he was nearing his retirement.

"C'mon in," the principal said when he heard the knock on the door. "Mike, have a seat. How's Joyce."

"That's what I wanted to talk to you about," Mr. Weber said and sat in the cushioned chair across the desk from his principal.

"What is it? Is she alright?" he asked.

"Well," Michael Weber said. "She was due last week, but the baby didn't come. The doctors want to give her a few more days before they induce. I have to be with her."

"Of course," Mr. Carnivali quickly agreed.

"That means I can't go on the field trip next week," he said. "I have to be home to take care of her and the baby. I'd like to go on paternity leave for a couple of weeks. I knowit's the worst time to take off from school, but her sister can't come out until the first of June."

"That's okay," his principal said. "We had three babies—I had to take off for a couple of weeks for the middle one. First things first."

"I'll be back for the final week of school and graduation," Mr. Weber said. "But I can't make the field trip next week."

"What about Dan Schneider?" Mr. Carnivali asked about the availability of the history teacher for the lower grades.

"He has that diocesan history competition for the kids on Friday—I already asked," he said. "Fr. Tom will be going with the bus," Mike said of the young assistant priest at the parish. "I have eight parent chaperones; we've raised the money and I've made all the reservations. The kids are really looking forward to it."

"Don't worry about it," Mr. Carnivali said. "You take care of your wife and baby. We'll figure it out."

"Thanks, Peter," Michael Weber said and got up to shake hands with his principal across the desk. "I'll fill out the request form and give it to Kathy by the end of the day. I'll give her the revised itinerary, too. Thanks, a lot." Mr. Weber left the office relieved to return to his next class.

Peter Carnivali was faced with another of the myriad personnel situations that crossed the desk of a Catholic school principal, especially with some younger, female faculty members having babies and beginning their family life. He looked at the picture of him and his wife and their three children when they were school age, hanging on the wall across the room. I had a good head of hair then, he thought. God bless Mike and Joyce with their first child, he prayed silently.

He flipped through his rolodex until he found the name of the dependable substitute teacher he had used throughout the school year to help cover the upper grades when needed. If I can get him to cover Mike's classes the next couple of weeks, Peter thought, all I have to do is find someone to lead the field trip. He called Mr. Kliner and left a message about the need for his help over the next two weeks. He might be subbing somewhere, he thought. I'll wait until the end of the day before I start looking for somebody else.

He quickly looked over the roster of his faculty to see if anyone seemed suitable to lead the field trip on short notice. In a modest-sized Catholic elementary school, there were not a lot of options. He buzzed the school secretary on the intercom.

"Yes, Mr. Carnivali," she answered.

"Kathy, if Joel Kliner calls," he explained, "I'm looking for him to substitute the next couple of weeks for Mike."

"I know," she interjected. "He and Joyce are having their first child. Isn't it wonderful! What about the eighth grade field trip?"

"I'm working on it," he said. "But first we have to secure a substitute. He usually calls by the end of the day."

Kathy and the faculty knew the Webers were expecting, but they did not know about the complications.

Peter Carnivali found the initial field trip itinerary among the papers scattered on his desk. A cursory scan of the day's schedule brought back memories of when he used to lead the field trip; it was basically the same as years ago. Mr. Weber had saved some time between Emmitsburg and Gettysburg by having a local bistro prepare boxed lunches for the forty or so pilgrims. They ate them during the twenty minutes it took to cross the Mason-Dixon Line into Pennsylvania. This innovation also allowed them to leave later in the morning for the hour-long bus ride to Emmitsburg, so the other school children could see them off. He had also added an initial stop at the new Gettysburg Visitors Center, which wasn't operational when he used to take the eighth graders. All-in-all, Mr. Weber had built upon the tradition that he had established at St. Thomas Aquinas Catholic School the previous years, and made the trip even better. Mr. Carnivali knew that the field trip was a kind of rite of passage for the eighth grade students in the year they made their Confirmation. I have to find the right person to lead the pilgrimage, he thought. It's their last adventure together as a class.

It didn't take long for the word to spread among the faculty and students that Mr. Weber would be unable to lead the trip. The eighth graders were concerned that after they had raised money through bake sales and car washes, they wouldn't be able to go on the trip that was the capstone of their final year in elementary school. Within the hour, Kathy buzzed Mr. Carnivali on the intercom. "It's Patty Wizneski for you. She's a little worked up."

"Put her on," Peter said, knowing that this year's PTG President's daughter, Melissa, was in the eighth grade class.

"How are you, Patty?" he said. "… Don't worry; they're still going … I know how much this means to the students…I realize that the PTG subsidizes half the cost of the trip… I have to find a competent employee to lead them … No, it has to be an employee of the school; it's an insurance matter … Don't worry, they're going next week, even if I have to take them myself … Please tell the parents that the pilgrimage is secure … Thank you. Good-bye."

When he hung up the phone, he realized that he was the ideal replacement for Mr. Weber to lead the trip. Afterall, I initiated this pilgrimage nearly twenty years ago. Who better to lead them than me? he thought.

Before he left school that day, Joel Kliner had returned Mr. Carnivali's call and confirmed his availability to substitute for Mr. Weber the next couple of weeks. As he drove home, he knew his wife might have some objections to his leading the field trip.

He thought about how he might approach her with the proposal. He knew that Alice had been anxiously looking forward to his retirement at the end of June, especially since his cardiologist had detected a mild heart murmur at his last visit.

Peter took off his sport coat and loosened his tie when he got home. He wanted to wait until after supper to broach the topic of the field trip with his wife. So, when they finished their stuffed chicken dinner and put the leftovers in the refrigerator, he poured himself a drink of his favorite single-malt scotch and settled into his easy chair. Alice joined him in the living room.

"I'm thinking about going on the eighth grade field trip next week, Alice," he said, tentatively. "Mike Weber's wife is experiencing some delay in delivering their baby and he's going on paternity leave for a couple of weeks." He watched as the expression on her face changed from relaxed to concerned, her eyes misting slightly.

"You know what Dr. Mellet said about not putting too much stress on your heart," Alice said with a certain trepidation.

"I know, dear," he said, "but the bus ride is only an hour to and from and Mike has the itinerary and reservations all worked out. I've done this trip more than a dozen times. It's not that bad."

"But it's all day," she countered, "from morning to evening. You know how the children can get ..." she trailed off.

He sipped his scotch. "Mike has eight chaperones," he reassured his wife of forty- three years. "And Fr. Thomas will be coming, too."

"Isn't there anybody else at school who can go?" Alice asked, realizing that once her husband had his mind made up, it was difficult to persuade him otherwise.

"The other teacher is tied up with some diocesan history competition that day," Peter explained. "I'll be alright. I've learned to pace myself."

"That's the problem," she said, her eyes misting, again. "With twenty-five kids, a dozen adults, and all that walking, you can't very well pace yourself. Unexpected things can happen."

He reached over to touch her hand on the arm of the couch where she was sitting.

"I'll be careful not to overdo it, Alice. This will be a kind of swan song for my years at Aquinas, my career in Catholic education. Pope Francis has declared this the Year of Mercy.

There's an indulgence given when you visit one of the designated churches. The Basilica of Saint Elizabeth Ann Seton in Emmitsburg has been designated as one of those pilgrimage sites," he said, relying on the religious aspect to convince his wife. "Maybe the trip will help my heart. God knows I could use His mercy."

Alice got up and sat on the arm of his easy chair to give her husband a hug. "What would I ever do if something happened to you?" she made her final appeal.

"Nothing is going to happen to me," he said to his wife and set down his glass. He embraced her in reassurance of his promise.

The next day at school, he went into Mr. Weber's homeroom first thing in the morning to tell him and his twenty-five students that he would lead their trip himself next week. While Mr. Weber looked relieved that his principal would assume the duty, the students' reaction was ambivalent. They were thrilled that their trip was secured with Mr. Carnivali, but they were skeptical about having their no-nonsense principal leading them. Afterall, Mr. Carnivali was the man who meted out detentions and, even suspensions, when they had gotten out of line over the years. And while he had the reputation of being fair, not harsh, they knew that they would not get away with much with him in charge of the trip.

The next week, the doctors induced Joyce Weber's labor on Tuesday and she delivered a healthy baby girl. Mr. Kliner was doing well substituting for Mr. Weber, as the students were familiar with him from the previous times he had subbed during the school year. Kathy double-checked all the plans for the trip, including the student roster with home phone numbers and allergies. The PTG was taking care of the boxed lunches, snacks, soda pop, and water. Mr. Carnivali reviewed the itinerary several times that week, being sure to have the phone numbers of the bus company, the Basilica Shrine, the Gettysburg Visitors' Center, and the Park Guide who would lead them through the battlefield, on his cell phone and on paper. More than once that week, Peter Carnivali said to himself, 'One more time,' as he grew excited with the prospect of the pilgrimage, his last hurrah. On Thursday he called Michael to check on his wife and baby, and had Kathy send a memorandom to the teachers with the good news, though most of them had already heard.

As he prepared to leave for the trip on Friday morning, Alice asked him if he had his nitroglycerin pills, just in case. He tapped his shirt pocket beneath his sport coat to signal to her that he was being cautious. After they kissed 'good-bye,' she straightened his tie and hugged him for a few extra seconds. "Don't be late," she said. "I'll be waiting."

"I'll call you when we're leaving Gettysburg, Alice," he said.

When he pulled up into the parking lot, he saw the bus idling near the main entrance of the school. A few cars were scattered in the lot, with some parents and students milling about. When he got out of his car, he checked the pocket of his sport coat, again, to be sure he had his cell phone. May's the ideal month to take a field trip, he thought. You can count on mild weather even if you have to endure larger crowds. He waved to the families as he went to meet the bus driver. Patricia Wiczneski and hear husband, Ralph, were already talking with the driver.

"Can we load our supplies in the bay?" Mr. Carnivali asked, after he had introduced himself and shook hands. "Let me open the hatches," the veteran driver said. Ralph and Patty began loading boxes from their van into the bottom of the bus: boxed lunches, snacks, and cans of soda pop and ice in styrofoam coolers, and a few cases of bottled water. Mr. Carnivali did not help in the loading, remembering his heart.

Some of the other parents of the eighth graders came over to help the Wiczneski's. Kathy came up to Mr. Carnivali and handed him a clipboard with the roster of students, chaperones, and phone numbers. He could see some of the other school students peeking out of their classroom windows on the second floor, envious of the eighth graders going on a field trip on a school day.

"Fr. Thomas," he greeted the young priest and extended his hand. "I'm glad you're joining us."

"I'm excited for the trip," the priest said. "This is my first visit back to Emmitsburg since I graduated. I went to seminary at Mount Saint Mary's, you know."

"You'll be sitting up front with me," Mr. Carnivali said. "Can you say a prayer before we leave? I'll hand you the microphone after I welcome everybody on board and give a few instructions."

"Of course," the young priest said, enthusiastically. "This is my first pilgrimage with our students—and in the Year of Mercy."

More cars started arriving with the eighth grade pilgrims. A few of the girls had small, shoulder bags, while others wore fanny packs in lieu of purses. No one needed a jacket on this warm May day.

Before they started boarding the coach, Kathy helped Mr. Carnivali line up the students. Most of the mothers, and some of the fathers, kissed their children 'goodbye,' as they sent them on this adventure beyond their supervision. Mr. Carnivali began to check off the names of the students and chaperones, all of whom he knew, as they boarded the bus. It only took about fifteen minutes to fill their coach.

"Is that everybody?" the bus driver said.

"Everybody except Bobby Murray," Mr. Carnivali said.

Just then, a pickup truck pulled into the parking lot and stopped near the bus.

Bobby Murray scrambled out of the truck and hurried over toward Mr. Carnivali.

"Bobby," Mr. Carnivali said in his authoritative principal's voice, and checked off his name on the roster.

"Good morning, Mr. Carnivali," Bobby said, in the most respectful voice he could muster, and went up the few steps into the idling bus. The saccharine tone of the boy's greeting brought a sardonic smile to the principal's face.

"All present and accounted for," Mr. Carnivali said to the bus driver, reminiscent of his years in the army reserve. He checked his watch: eight-forty-five a.m. Right on time.

Mr. Carnivali sat in the front seat near the window, with an empty seat next to him where he set his sport coat and the small bag of fruit that Alice had packed him. Fr. Thomas sat across the aisle in the seat behind the driver. He set his breviary on the empty seat next to him, as well as a book he was reading about preaching.

He planned to use the bus rides to pray and read. He had prepared his homily for today's Mass, yesterday. Once Peter could see that everyone was settled in their seats and ready to go, he took the micro- phone that was hanging behind the driver's seat and stood up to address the pilgrims.

"Good morning, everyone," he started. "It's been several years since I went on the eighth grade field trip. As you already know, Mr. Weber's wife, Joyce, delivered their baby girl this week. We have eight parent chaperones with us today, Fr. Thomas, and myself, so if you get sick or need something, please find one of us to help. When we're at the shrine or the battlefield, stay with our group. Do not go wondering off by yourself or with another classmate. There will be a lot of other students out there today. Mr. Weber has planned our day with his usual precision, giving us both time to see everything, as well as to keep us moving. Let's have a good time today and enjoy this last excursion of your years at St. Thomas Aquinas School." When he finished, he handed the microphone to Fr. Thomas.

A few of the parents began clapping when they remembered that Mr. Carnivali would be retiring at the end of June. Then the whole bus, parents and students, broke out in a thunderous round of applause for their longtime principal. Some of the students began to cheer and shout, but he couldn't determine why they were cheering, exactly. Was it a salute for his years of service or an outburst of relief that he was leaving?

When the clapping stopped, Fr. Thomas stood to offer a simple prayer for the intercession of St. Thomas Aquinas and St. Elizabeth Ann Seton to protect them on the drive to and from their destinations and throughout their pilgrimage. He ended with an invocation to the Holy Spirit to fill the hearts of these recently confirmed Catholic boys and girls as they prepared to enter a new phase of their lives in high school. Concluding the prayer with the traditional trinitarian blessing, he replaced the microphone in its holder behind the bus driver.

"Wagons ho!" Mr. Carnivali said in an old, western expression lost on most everyone except the driver, who promptly pulled the bus out of the school parking lot. They were on their way.

The short drive to Emmitsburg, Maryland, from Harrisburg took less than an hour. With no bathroom or food stops, they would arrive at the Basilica in plenty of time for Fr. Thomas to vest and celebrate the ten o'clock Mass scheduled for the school. Mr. Weber had previously designated certain students to do the readings, responsorial psalm, and petitions, while he also had selected two of the boys to be the altar servers. There was nothing for Mr. Carnivali to do but sit back and enjoy the scenic drive on this beautiful May day, so he loosened his tie. He had lived in Pennsylvania all of his life and had always enjoyed the lush forests and plentiful streams and lakes found in the commonwealth.

He recalled how he and Alice had taken their children on numerous weekend camping trips while they still enjoyed outings with their parents. Once they all became teenagers, they seemed to find excuses for why they couldn't go camping with the family anymore.

He looked in the brownbag that Alice has prepared for him. There were a couple Chambersburg peaches and some local apples. The peaches were not quite in season yet, so he took an apple and offered the fruit to Fr. Thomas who had just set down his breviary following mid-morning prayer.

"Thanks," the young priest said and selected one of the peaches from the bag along with a napkin.

The principal and priest sat comfortably in their front seats, oblivious to the shenanigans the students were plotting, content to eat their fruit and let the driver transport their entourage to holy ground. The presence of the chaperones seated throughout the bus kept the students reasonably quiet. When he finished the apple, he wrapped the core in his napkin and tossed it into the garbage bag hanging at the front of the bus. Then Mr. Carnivali sat back, closed his eyes, and tried to get a few minutes of rest before the bedlam began.

Fr. Thomas silently rehearsed his homily from the notecards he had prepared yesterday. He was looking forward to celebrating Mass in the magnificent Basilica.

"We just crossed the Mason-Dixon Line," the bus driver said over his shoulder to Mr. Carnivali. "We're in Maryland, now."

Peter opened his eyes, collecting his thoughts, and tightened his tie. Then he got up to address his passengers and raised the microphone to his mouth. "We just crossed the Mason-Dixon Line into Maryland," he said. "As you may know, the name derives from the two English surveyors who mapped the border between Pennsylvania and Maryland in the eighteenth century. They used the stars in the heavens to chart the boundaries on the earth." He used the turn of phrase that he had developed over the years, confident that none of them had heard it before. He paused and braced himself against the pole near his seat when the bus hit a bump in the road. "It also served as the demarcation between the slave and free states before abolition."

He put on his gray sport coat and sat down for a while. When he saw the dome of the Basilica, he got back up to address the pilgrims. "When the bus drops us off, follow Fr. Thomas up into the Basilica, don't dilly-dally. Mass is at ten sharp. Don't forget to shut off your cell phones. The docent will meet us at the door and direct us to the pews in the front of the church."

When the driver stopped the bus and opened the doors, Mr. Carnivali got out and stood at the bottom of the stairs with his clipboard. As each student stepped out of the bus, he checked off their names. When the last chaperone couple came out, Patty and Ralph Wiczneski, he asked them if they had seen Bobby Murray.

"Someone was still in the bathroom," Ralph said. "I knocked on the door and told them to hurry up."

When Bobby finally came off the bus, Mr. Carnivali said just loud enough for him hear: "So, it's going to be like that, hunh."

The bus driver told the principal that he would park the bus on the other side of the lot to meet them after Mass and the tour of the buildings and grounds.

Most of the adults and all of the students had never been in the Basilica before today. Saint Elizabeth Ann Seton was the first American-born saint, and all of the bishops in the United States had contributed to its magnificent construction in honor of the patroness of Catholic education. As the docent welcomed them to their pews, they were gawking at the high dome and beautiful murals decorating the church. There was a light, fresh look to the interior, though the architectural design was similar to the older, more imposing European basilicas.

Fr. Thomas headed for the sacristy along with the two altar servers. The sacristan directed the priest to the white vestments for the Solemnity and the boys to their albs and cinctures. The nun had everything set out for the Mass. Fr. Thomas vested and signed the opened Mass book on the countertop.

Meanwhile, Mr. Carnivali led the four students who were going to read the Old Testa- ment excerpt, the responsorial psalm, the epistle, and the petitions, to the ambo to familiarize them with their parts for Mass. Once he thought they were ready, he led them back to the front pew and sat them in order so that he could cue them to go forward when their time came. Within a few minutes, a server rang the bell to signal the beginning of Mass.

They all stood at the sound of the bell. A few locals joined them for the morning liturgy. Fr. Thomas began at the altar with the opening blessing and greeting for the Solemnity of the Most Sacred Heart of Jesus, as designated in the liturgical calendar. He offered the penitential rite, to which the pilgrims responded: "Lord, have mercy; Christ, have mercy; Lord, have mercy." He led them in the recitation of the 'Gloria.' Then he prayed the collect. When the priest sat down in the presider's chair, flanked by the servers, Mr. Carnivali prompted the class president to get up and do the first reading.

"A reading from the prophet, Ezekiel," the boy began at the lectern. He read, in a clear voice, the passage about God assuring His chosen people that He would shepherd them Himself and tend His flock, rescuing them from darkness and leading them to good pastures where they would find rest. And finally, that He would seek out the lost, and bring back the strays. "The word of the Lord," the reader concluded. When he returned to the pew, Mr. Carnivali prompted the vice-president to do the responsorial psalm.

"The Lord is my shepherd, there is nothing I shall want," the girl announced the familiar refrain and raised her hand to encourage their response. Again, the twenty-third psalm assured His people of God's guidance and protection, leading them to refreshing waters, encouraging them to fear no evil, and to dwell in the house of the Lord. When she finished and returned, Mr. Carnivali told the next reader to rise.

"A reading from Paul's letter to the Romans," the tall boy began in his resounding voice. The apostle assured the disciples that their hope does not disappoint because God has poured out the Holy Spirit into their hearts through the salvific cross of Jesus Christ and his glorious resurrection. When the tall boy came down the steps of the sanctuary, he stumbled slightly, causing some of the students to giggle.

Mr. Carnivali, nonetheless, was pleased that they had all read with good diction and understanding.

Fr. Thomas rose and intoned the 'Alleluia,' the first singing in the Mass. The pilgrims rose to echo the familiar chant.

At the pulpit, he greeted the people and declared the gospel selection from the evangelist, Luke. He read the parable of the lost sheep, describing how the shepherd goes after the lost one until he finds it, and then celebrates with his neighbors.

All the pilgrims sat down in their pews to listen to the young priest's homily.

Fr. Thomas had earned the reputation of engaging the students at the school masses.

"I want to congratulate all of you for making the effort to come on this pilgrimage in this Year of Mercy as declared by Pope Francis. The Holy Spirit of God accompanies you on this field trip, which is both a spiritual and historical adventure," Fr. Thomas began, as he looked out over the thirty-five pilgrims and the dozen other locals who joined them. "I know it's also a day to get out of school as you near your graduation, but there is much to learn and experience as we straddle the Mason-Dixon Line between Emmitsburg and Gettysburg. Our Lord has been shepherding you these past several years, with His merciful heart, as you have advanced through St. Thomas Aquinas Elementary School, and today, leads you to good pastures and restful waters where you will find refreshment for your souls."

One of the chaperones nudged Bobby Murray on the back of his shoulder because the boy was slumped over, having fallen asleep during the homily.

From the corner of his eye, Mr. Carnivali saw Bobby straighten up in his pew. He knew about the rough home life of his eighth grader. His natural father, who was not married to Bobby's mother, was in jail for another drunk driving charge. His mother was living with a man who only worked seasonally. Mr. Carnivali had helped her meet the tuition payments with generous grants from the scholarship fund. He already has two strikes against him, he thought. He had suspended Bobby in the Fall for fighting, and had given him numerous detentions for misbehavior. Though he was a bright enough student, at times, he was out of control. He was always crossing the line. If it wasn't for Mr. Weber's help, he may not have been able to graduate, he thought. As it is, one more incident and I might have to hold back his diploma and expel him. Bobby Murray is a lost sheep if there ever was one, he mused.

"Throughout the day, I want you to learn about three people: a saint, a priest, and a soldier, who will figure prominently on our pilgrimage," Fr. Thomas continued his spirited homily.

"First, Saint Elizabeth Ann Seton, in whose Basilica we celebrate this Mass. A teacher, a wife, a mother of five, a widow, a convert to Catholicism who suffered persecution in New York until she found a safe haven for her family in Maryland, and, then, a religious foundress of the Daughters of Charity—the same nuns who would nurse the wounded at the Battle of Gettysburg. Her life should be especially of interest to our girls."

"Second," he continued. "Fr. William Corby, Catholic chaplain at the battle who, with cannon fire exploding and bullets whizzing by him, stood up to administer general absolution to the soldiers of the Irish Brigade out of New York, who were rushing to reinforce the Union line at Seminary Ridge, and who went on to become the President of Notre Dame University after the war."

"And third, Colonel Joshua Chamberlain, a Protestant, of the Twentieth Maine, whose quick thinking and heroic actions inspired his battalion at the Battle of Little Round Top to thwart the Confederate soldiers trying to flank the Union position and, possibly, collapse the Union line."

He grew more animated as he reached his conclusion. "All three of these people, whose legacy you will learn about today, had a deep faith in God and trusted Him to lead them through the dark valleys of life. Learn from their example. Learn about their heroic virtue and trust in God's providential care to deliver them from the trials and tribulations they encountered in their lives."

"While their roles were different, their faith in God's love for them never wavered and enabled them to follow His will whatever the challenge. In the end, they all led victorius lives that made an impact on the people around them and earned them a place in American history, and, we pray, in heaven." The young priest paused at the pulpit, letting his final words hang in the cavernous Basilica over the pilgrims.

Going back to the presider's chair, Fr. Thomas led the pilgrims in the Creed and then introduced the petitions. The student rose to read them at Mr. Carnivali's prompting.

The intercessions were a combination of the few provided by the Sacristan and a couple that Mr. Carnivali added for the safety of the pilgrims and the health and well-being of Joyce and Michael Weber and their newborn baby.

A couple of the students brought up the gifts of bread and wine from the table at the front pew and handed them to Fr. Thomas who, in turn, handed them to the servers. During the offertory, preface, and eucharistic prayer, the students were appropriately attentive, seemingly touched by the priest's sermon. At the consecration, they focused on the bread and wine transformed into the body and blood of Jesus Christ through the power of the Holy Spirit. They were all deeply familiar with the Catholic understanding of the Mass.

The pilgrims, as a body, prayed the Lord's Prayer with mature conviction as they prepared to receive communion. As they had done hundreds of times in their young lives, they approached the priest for 'The

Body of Christ,' to which they responded, 'Amen,' prior to reception.

After the closing prayer, Mr. Carnivali got up to remind the eighth graders to stay in their pews after Mass for the docent, who would lead them in a brief history and tour of the Basilica. Fr. Thomas then concluded the pilgrimage liturgy with the final Trinitarian blessing and commissioning of those in attendance.

As the docent began her talk about the life of St. Elizabeth Ann Seton, Mr. Carnivali slipped into the sacristy to hand a folded fifty dollar bill to Fr. Thomas, who slid it into the empty envelope near the Mass book as an offering. Some things never change, Mr. Carnivali thought. Meanwhile, the two altar servers joined their classmates in the pews. The docent, a lay woman, let the students and chaperones know that a short film, a small museum, and a bookstore awaited them downstairs in the crypt. She encouraged the students to pray the formal prayers designated to obtain the plenary indulgence for pilgrims visiting the Basilica in this Year of Mercy. In answer to a student's question, the docent explained that a plenary indulgence was the removal of all of the temporal punishment due to sin. She also told them that a brief instruction about the prayers could be found on a laminated card near the tomb of St. Elizabeth Ann Seton, which they would have the opportunity to visit and venerate when she was finished. The docent then pointed out some of the distinctive architectural and artistic features of the Basilica before reminding the class that every bishop in the United States raised money in the nineteen-sixties to build this beautiful house of God in honor of the first American-born saint. Mr. Carnivali and Fr. Thomas returned to the pews just before she directed the pilgrims to reverently explore the church and say the prayers to obtain the indulgence.

Then, Mr. Carnivali told his students to meet him in the vestibule in about twenty minutes where there was both an elevator and stairway to go down to the crypt to see the movie and museum about the saint's life.

The twenty-five students and the chaperones moved about the church, took the time to pray to obtain the plenary indulgence, and were in awe of the Basilica, the largest church that most of them had ever seen. The chaperones had to remind the students, more than once, to keep their voices to a whisper out of respect for this impressive church where a saint is buried.

When they gathered in the vestibule after a while, some of them used the bathroom facilities while others followed Mr. Carnivali down the steps to the crypt. Fr. Thomas and a couple of the chaperones took some students on the elevator down to the lower level, while other chaperones waited for the last students to come out of the lavatories. Their group nearly filled the small theatre to watch the short film about the fascinating life of St. Elizabeth Ann Seton. After a brief introduction by one of the sisters, most of the students became interested in the film with its good acting and period costumes. They had already learned a little about her life from Mr. Weber in preparation for the Pilgrimage.

When the movie was finished, the sister encouraged them to explore the Seton Museum and the bookstore across the hall. A group of the eighth grade girls moved together along the wall display to read the highlights of her life and view the drawings of her and some of the objects of significance before she became a nun, such as her ballet slippers and her wedding dress. Fr. Thomas and some students moved ahead to other displays that interested them. The chaperones distributed themselves among the students, mindful of the glass display cases.

Peter Carnivali took the opportunity to slip into the bookstore and buy something for his wife, Alice. He walked around the store until he saw a display case with a variety of rosaries. He knew, then, what he would buy her. Her rosaries were a bit worn due to her deep devotion to the Blessed Virgin Mary and her habit of prayer. More than once he had to use her tweezers to refasten the delicate links of the chain holding the blue beads together.

"So, what color is that pair?" he asked the volunteer behind the counter, pointing to the rough cut beads of a purple hue.

"That's amethyst," she said. "I have a pair myself," and took them out of the display case to give him a better look.

"I'll take that one," he said, knowing Alice would love the violet stone and, even more, that he bought them for her while he was on pilgrimage with the students. He handed her the money and she put the rosaries in a small plastic box and then in a paper bag.

"For my wife," he said and took his change and gift bag.

When he came out of the shop, he could see that many of the students and chaperones were gathering at the door of the crypt, ready to move on to the next station on the tour. Calling out to the others who were lingering near the museum displays, Mr. Carnivali waited until he saw the last of them join the other pilgrims.

"Follow me," he said as he moved to the front of their large group and out of the double doors of the Basilica crypt. A wave of nostalgia passed over him as he wondered how many times he had led eighth grade students out of those doors and onto the grounds of the shrine site. He crossed a street toward a small, white house about a hundred yards away, with his entourage of students and chaperones behind him. The May sun was warm; Mr. Carnivali wiped his face with his handkerchief.

They were met at the door by another docent who asked them to walk through this replica of Mother Seton's original school house and home for her five children, in groups of about ten, or so, so as not to become congested in the narrow hallways and small rooms.

When they had all seen the first floor classroom and kitchen, Mr. Carnivali led them on a path across the lawn toward a larger building that housed her family, her nuns, and the students as her school and order grew.

He stopped at a large, stone marker that explained that Union soldiers had crossed the property on their way to Gettysburg, with the sisters praying that the impending battle not take place on their grounds.

Another docent welcomed them at the door and showed them to the chapel where Mother Seton prayed before the Blessed Sacrament. The classroom, the dining room, and the parlor with an old, pedal-driven sewing machine and a piano, were considerably larger than the original residence, but the desks and chairs were still small by contem- porary standards. While the children felt freer to talk in these rooms, the chaperones urged them to keep their conversations in a quiet voice. Once outside, Mr. Carnivali walked them through the adjacent cemetery, the final resting place of her Daughters of Charity and two of her own children who died while they were young. Mr. Carnivali pointed out the gravestone of Mother Seton before she was canonized a saint and her body exhumed and placed in the Basilica a generation ago. The students all gathered on a landing between two sets of concrete steps overlook- ing the cemetery for a group photograph. A few of the chaperones took pictures with their cell phone cameras, until one of them invited Mr. Carnivali and Fr. Thomas to join them for the picture. Dutifully, they stood at the bottom of the staircases, with Mr. Carnivali clutching his gift bag, as the chaperones took more pictures. Peter Carnivali reminisced about the many times he had posed with his students, here, in past years. When they had taken sufficient pictures of the twenty-five smiling students with their principal and priest, the students descended the stairs and Mr. Carnivali walked them across the lawn and street toward their bus, which was parked on the far side of the Basilica lot. As the pilgrims made their way, he mentioned to Patty and Ralph Wiczneski to go ahead with some of the chaperones to get ready to pass out the boxed lunches and beverages as the students boarded the bus.

At the bus, Mr. Carnivali got his clipboard and began checking the names of the students as they boarded with their food and drink. The process went well; the students were hungry and thirsty. The chaperones handed out the boxed lunches and choice of drinks, bottled water or cans of soda pop, to each student without event, careful to take notice of the dietary restrictions, like glutenfree and peanut oil, written on the box.

Bobby Murray was one of the last to board with his lunch and can of soda.

"So, how did you like it, Bobby?" Mr. Carnivali said.

"It was alright," he said. "But I can't wait to go to the battlefield."

"Of course," Mr. Carnivali said, under his breath, as he checked off his name.

The chaperones gave the principal a lunch and a bottle of water. When he stepped up into the bus, he saw that Fr. Thomas was already seated with his opened lunch box on his lap. A chaperone gave a lunch and water to the bus driver which he gladly accepted.

The last chaperones brought the few extra lunches on board, while another carried a half-empty case of water.

"Could you say grace before the wolves devour their meal?" Mr. Carnivali asked Fr. Thomas.

"Of course," the priest said. He stood facing the pilgrims and held the microphone to his face. He offered a simple thanksgiving for the food, the hands that prepared it, and the completion of the first half of their pilgrimage.

With that, everyone opened their boxed lunches, finding a sandwich, a piece of fruit, chips or pretzels, and a cookie. The bus pulled out of the Basilica parking lot, with the driver waiting for the stop in Gettysburg before having his lunch. The air conditioning kept the coach nice and cool while they ate. Mr. Carnivali took the microphone reminding the students that the ride to Gettysburg would take about twenty minutes, so be certain to eat quickly and not fuss. While there was a little trading of snacks and fruit, the bus was already quiet with most everyone enjoying their moveable feast.

As they finished their lunch, Fr. Thomas asked Mr. Carnivali about his upcoming retirement.

"How do you feel after all these years?" he said.

"Well, I won't miss the paperwork," he said. "It's grown exponentially over the years. But I will miss the kids and many of the teachers, especially the younger ones that I mentored." He paused a moment, reflecting on his career. "Having a hand in the spiritual and intellectual development of so many students has been a wonderful experience. I wouldn't trade it for anything in the world. And the fact that I may have helped to shape the careers of the next generation of some of our teachers in Catholic education is very gratifying."

"You've done a great job," the young priest said. "You're respected across the diocese."

"Maybe," he said. "But mostly I hope I've earned the respect of the families I served. These days, they need all the support they can get."

"That's for sure," Fr. Thomas concurred.

Sooner than they expected, their bus pulled up in front of the new Gettysburg Visitors Center to unload the pilgrims. Mr. Carnivali took the microphone to remind them to take their garbage with them when they left the bus. Mr. and Mrs. Wiczneski held two large plastic garbage bags at the bottom of the steps, so that the students could dispose of their boxes and papers in one, and their bottles and cans in the other before they entered the Center. A few of the other chaperones walked through the bus after the students left to pick up any leftover bottles, bags, or papers. Mr. Carnivali asked Fr. Thomas to lead the students directly to the first floor movie theatre where they would line up for the one o'clock showing, while he waited to herd the last of them. Once they were all in the serpentine line set off with stanchions and velvet ropes, Mr. Carnivali moved to the front to identify his group for the attendants and give them the thirty-five tickets for each of the pilgrims. When an earlier group of students left, they were let into the theatre and took their seats for the film. Within a few minutes, the lights went down and the movie began.

Popular actor Morgan Freeman narrated the film depicting the Battle of Gettysburg, the furthest incursion of the Confederate army across the Mason-Dixon Line into the northern states. The well-made documentary held the pilgrims' interest. For Mr. Carnivali, Fr. Thomas, and most of the chaperones, this was also the first time that they had seen the movie, though it had aired on the public broadcasting station last year The nearly hour-long film provided the viewers with a full account of the battle, the grounds, and the pivotal importance of Gettysburg in light of the entire Civil War.

When the movie was over, the lights went on, and they were directed by a voice on the loudspeaker to exit to the left and take the elevator or escalator up to the second level where they would see the Cyclorama, the nineteenth-century, circular, depiction of the battle. Mr. Carnivali waited outside of the theatre with his clipboard to be sure that they didn't lose anyone in transition.

"Bobby," Mr. Carnivali said when the adolescent was among the last to leave.

"Mr. Carnivali," the boy said, aware that his principal had his eye on him.

The Cyclorama was a three-hundred-sixty degree painting that portrayed the battle before the invention of motion pictures. The aide explained that lights and sounds would go off on various parts of the circular painting in coordination with the narration to simulate live action. The adults and most of the students found the Cyclorama interesting as a necessary stage before the advent of movies, while others were bored as they had been spoiled by modern cinematography. Over the loudspeaker, the audience was in- formed that this display had been housed in Boston until the recent building of the Visitors Center. Afterwards, they were instructed to go back downstairs to tour the museum and bookstore, and find the café and lavatories.

As they descended one way or another, Mr. Carnivali instructed the chaperones to spread out among the various groups of their students and remind them to meet in the lobby at three o'clock to board the bus and begin the guided battlefield tour. While all of this was new to him, too, Mr. Carnivali had a honed talent for keeping packs of unruly teenagers in good order after decades of experience in Catholic schools. The challenge here was that there were hundreds of other school children throughout the Center, as Gettysburg was one of the most popular destinations in Pennsylvania for school field trips. Walking through the museum, Mr. Carnivali recognized some of the items and displays that had been previously kept at various sites around Gettysburg until the new Visitors Center was built a few years ago. He had seen cannons, swords, rifles, uniforms, and saddles from his earlier school trips but, now, appreciated the skillfulness with which they were gathered and arranged in this new museum to further deepen tourists' awareness of warfare one-hundred-fifty years ago. How much better this is than the Wax Museum, he thought. He watched as some of his eighth grade students stopped to read the panels explaining certain aspects of the Civil War.

When he completed the museum tour, he went to the lavatory and, then, to the bookstore to browse. Among the crowd shopping, he saw some of his students in line at the cashiers' counter with various items. He spotted Bobby Murray near a display of Civil War soldiers and moved closer to his aisle, but not too close. He could see boxes of the toy soldiers stacked up in the aisle about the size of a board game but a little thicker.

Bobby seemed fascinated with the display of plastic soldiers, cannons, horses, and flags. In the midst of the
crowded store, Mr. Carnivali saw Bobby place one of
the boxed sets under his arm and attempt to walk toward the door. But the roving store manage con-
fronted the boy trying to steal the battlefield set.

"Wait up, Bobby," Mr. Carnivali said as he quickly
walked toward them. "I found my wallet," he said to
the manager and handed him two twenty dollar bills.
"Is that enough?"

Bobby looked at Mr. Carnivali with astonishment.

"We'll need a bag, too," the principal said.

Though he was a little skeptical, the manager accepted the explanation and went to a cashier to ring up
the purchase. The set cost twenty-nine dollars and
ninety-nine cents, plus tax. Mr. Carnivali took his
change and walked out of the gift shop with Bobby.

"Go catch up with the others," he said to the boy and
patted him on the back.

Bobby walked away dumbfounded, clutching the
battlefield set under his arm. Once the students were all
accounted for in the vestibule, Mr. Carnivali directed
them back onto the bus that was idling near the exit.
The driver had eaten his lunch and disposed of the
garbage bags while they were in the Center. Again, Mr.
Carnivali checked off their names on his clipboard roster as they stepped up into the coach. When Bobby
Murray boarded holding his package, he averted his

eyes from Mr. Carnivali. The bus drive stopped at the end of the parking lot to pick up the battlefield tour guide, an older, bespeckled man in a tan park uniform with a wide-brimmed ranger's hat.

When the guide and Mr. Carnivali saw each other, they both let out a mild exclamation and shook hands.

"I see you're still at it, Al," Mr. Carnivali said.

"How many years has it been, Pete?" the guide asked.

"At least a half-dozen," Mr. Carnivali said. "I let their history teacher pick up the field trip a while back. But this year, his wife just had a baby so I'm filling in on my last rodeo. I'm retiring next month." The bus pulled out of the parking lot. "I thought about it myself," the guide said as he took the seat next to Mr. Carnivali. "But I'm having too much fun. Speaking of which, I better get started." He stood up and set what looked like a doctor's black, medical bag on the seat. He took off his hat and placed it atop the bag. He told the bus driver to make a right turn at the stop sign and grabbed the microphone.

"Good afternoon, everyone," he said. "My name is Alfred Rawlings and I'll be your battlefield guide today. I've been doing this for over thirty years. Your principal and I go way back, to when he was just a young history teacher."

Some of the boys snickered at the suggestion that their balding principal was ever a young man. "You have fair weather, today," Mr. Rawlings said. "The good Lord must be smiling on you. Before we go to the battlefield, I want to show you something that should be of interest to your group." He told the driver to make a right turn at the traffic light and head into town. He leaned toward Mr. Carnivali and said: "I take it you're coming up from Emmitsburg?"

"That's right," the principal answered.

The guide told the bus driver to make a left turn and pull up in the middle of the block. When the bus was double parked, he spoke again, into the microphone: "St. Francis Xavier Catholic Church was built in 1831, well before the Civil War. Let's get out here and go inside." He hung up the microphone.

Mr. Carnivali, clipboard in hand, led the pilgrims out of the bus and toward the steps to the front door. Once the students and chaperones were all in the Church, Mr. Rawlings motioned to them to come closer to the front where he was standing. "Take a look around and imagine this Church as the field hospital for the Battle of Gettysburg," he projected his voice and waved his arm. "They put wooden planks across pews to make beds for the thousands of soldiers injured during the three days of the fighting. The Daughters of Charity, Mother Elizabeth Ann Seton's sisters, came from Emmitsburg to nurse the wounded and dying soldiers from both the Union and Confederate armies. It was a messy business, the floor soaked with the blood of the brave men fighting for their beliefs, many of them not much older than you." For a few minutes, he let the pilgrims imagine this house of God turned into a hospital emergency ward.

"Now, take a look at that stained glass window on your right nearest the sanctuary," he pointed. "It depicts the Daughters of Charity, in full habit, nursing the wounded soldiers. You'll notice there's both a Union and Confederate flag in that window, which was installed years later as a tribute to the men and women who sacrificed so much in this historic battle. Mr. Carnivali always loved this initial stop on the tour, as it illustrated the intersection of both American and Catholic history that was the purpose of the pilgrimage. He encouraged the students to take a closer look at the colorful, stained glass window.

When everyone had the opportunity to look more closely at the artistic depiction, he led them back out of the Church.

Mr. Carnivali, again, checked off the roster of names on his clipboard as they boarded the bus. The mood of the pilgrims was more somber, now, as the sober reality of warfare settled on the teenagers. Mr. Rawlings directed the driver out of town toward the battlefield.

"As we pass through what used to be a peach orchard, imagine hundreds of confederate troops advancing through the trees on the Union position," he said into the microphone. "If you look out of the left side of the bus, you can see a large hole in the side of that barn about a hundred yards away. That was made by Confederate cannon fire and left there by the townsfolk as an historical reminder of the battle."

He opened up his black bag and pulled out an inactive cannon ball to reinforce his point. Holding it up for all to see, he said: "I'll pass this around so all of you can have a better feel for the weapons of war in the mid-nineteenth century. Please pass it down this side and back up the other. Be careful; it's heavy."

Mr. Carnivali always appreciated the extra things that Mr. Rawlings kept in his bag to help make the battle more real for the students. He was also happy to relinquish direction of this part of their field trip to the guide as he was feeling a little tired, anyhow. "As we go up here aways," Mr. Rawlings said to the pilgrims, "you'll note some headstones in random places in the fields. Just last year they unearthed the skeletal remains of a union soldier while repairing the bridge." When the cannonball was eventually passed forward, Mr. Rawlings placed it back in his black bag.

While the guide continued pointing out various battlefield highlights as the bus followed the familiar route, Mr. Carnivali remembered a random incident that occurred on one of his early pilgrimages with the students. An adolescent girl, with sugar diabetes, fell into a near coma on the bus when her blood sugar level fell dangerously low and she faced a serious health risk. Fortunately, one of the chaperones had been a nurse, who recognized the symptoms and had the girl drink some soda pop and eat a candybar to raise her level quickly. From that point on, Mr. Carnivali was always certain to have a health professional on the bus in case of any emergencies. He wondered if Mr. Weber had continued the practice. Then, Mr. Rawlings directed the bus driver to turn up a winding, tree-lined road and pull over at the crest of the hill, behind another bus that was already parked and letting off students.

Mr. Carnivali and Mr. Rawlings, clipboard and black bag in-hand, respectively, were the first to depart the coach. While they were out in the afternoon sun, here it was a little cooler because of the tall, dense tree cover that shrouded the site. Albert Rawlings, with his hat on, marched the pilgrims to the place where the Confederate troops gathered beneath the trees to launch the infamous Pickett's Charge across the mile-long, open field to attack the Union army on Seminary Ridge. He waited for the students and chaperones to take their positions among the half-dozen cannons that marked the clearing. Mr. Carnivali leaned against the wheel of one of the cannons. Once they were settled, the guide began the spiel that he had used hundreds of times before.

"Following a barrage of cannon fire on the Union position along Seminary Ridge, General Lee had devised a plan whereby thousands of his troops would march across the open field, converging at the center of the Union line, marked by a copse of trees, in the hopes of splitting the Union army. It was a bold and daring military maneuver that, if successful, could have turned the tide of the battle. He entrusted his most accomplished field officer, General George Pickett, to spearhead the attack. Mr. Rawlings paused, for effect, letting the conflict form in the imaginations of his keen listeners.

"Meanwhile, the Union soldiers were unleashing their own barrage of cannon fire and rifle volleys on the advancing Rebel army. You can imagine what happened next," he paused, again. "Hundreds of Confederate soldiers were killed or lay wounded in the open field as their brave comrades continued their relentless march to the copse of trees on Seminary Ridge. Then, he stopped to pull out a small, hand saw from his black bag. "Recall our earlier stop at the St. Francis Xavier Church that was turned into a battlefield hospital. Do any of you know what this was used for?" He held up the saw for them to see.

A boy raised his hand slowly, until Mr. Rawlings pointed to him. "To cut off the arms and legs of the wounded soldiers," he said.

A muffled gasp rose among the others.

"Precisely!" Mr. Rawlings declared. "With not much more than a mouthful of whiskey and roll of cloth to clench between their teeth, these valiant soldiers bore the pain of having their limbs amputated by this crude instrument of surgery." He let the pilgrims catch their breath.

"And while a few of their comrades did reach the copse, in the end, thousands of other Confederate soldiers lay dead or wounded in that field of blood," he continued dramatically. "General Lee's daring gambit failed to win the day and, what was left of his scattered troops, returned to the cover of these trees, defeated and demoralized."

Mr. Carnivali found himself captivated by the guide's polished retelling of the battle, though he had heard and read about it dozens of times before.

Mr. Rawlings then led the pilgrims on a short walk to the famous statue of General Robert E. Lee atop his trusted steed, Traveler. Some of the pilgrims took pictures on their cell phones of their classmates near the base of the popular monument.

When the last of the pictures were taken, Mr. Carnivali and Fr. Thomas led them back to their coach. Dutifully, the principal checked off their names on his clipboard roster as they boarded. All present and accounted for, he thought, as he followed Mr. Rawlings onto the bus. The air conditioned coach was a cool relief from the hot May sun. The chaperones passed out the remaining bottles of water to anyone who was thirsty. The bus driver continued onto the next major stop as indicated by the tour guide. They drove for several minutes. Then, Mr. Rawlings took the microphone, again, and began preparing the pilgrims for the unusual up-coming site. He was already planning to let the students get out to explore the rock formations. "Up here aways is Devil's Den and, as you will understand, sharp-shooters hid all through the rocks with their rifles aimed at enemy soldiers. It was a kind of stronghold from where the Confederates could control the surrounding fields and limit the Union's movements." He told the driver to park in the small lot at the end of the road. "We'll give you about twenty minutes to get out and climb among the large rocks, some of them bigger than this bus. Be careful," he said.

When they stopped, Mr. Carnivali took the micro-phone to remind the students to be back on the bus in twenty minutes. He and Fr. Thomas waited at the bottom of the steps as the young people came out and headed for the rock formations. Most of the adults stayed on or close to the bus, not risking the rough and uneven contours of Devil's Den.

The teenagers spread out in small groups to explore the large boulders and the spaces between them. The rock formation was so unusual that it almost appeared to be unearthly, like something one would see in a science fiction movie on the surface of another planet. It did not take long for some of the more adventurous boys to start climbing the largest boulders. Mr. Carnivali, Fr. Thomas, and the other chaperones watched the students scrambling atop the rocks. After a while, they could see Bobby Murray standing and waving from the top of the largest boulder like he had just scaled Mount Everest. Then, they watched as he slipped momentarily, his black hair disheveled, until he regained his balance and started his descent, a full twenty feet below. Mr. Carnivali just shook his head and prayed that they all came back in one piece. As they reboarded the bus, Mr. Carnivali checked off their names on his clipboard roster. Bobby Murray was the last to get on the bus.

"The last shall be first," Mr. Carnivali said.

"And the first shall be last," Bobby said, glancing at his principal. "I know that one." The tour guide directed the bus driver to follow the road behind Devil's Den. When they came to a large field bordered by trees, their guide had the bus stop.

"This is the Wheatfield," Mr. Rawlings began into the microphone, "the site of some of the bloodiest fighting in Gettysburg, where hundreds of soldiers died. Shielded by the trees, they shot at each other all day. And when the South tried to advance on the Union position, they were shot down in the field. And if the North tried to attack Confederates, they were gunned down beside the enemy soldiers." He paused to let the pilgrims imagine the field filled with bodies. "By the end of the day of fighting, both sides suffered hundreds of casualties, let alone the wounded." When he finished his account, he told the bus driver to follow the road back out for about ten minutes to the approach of Little

Roadtop. The bus driver was familiar with most of the battlefield highlights, as he had taken dozens of tour groups to Gettysburg over the years.

Mr. Rawlings took his seat next to Mr. Carnivali to rest a while. "You look a little tired, Pete," he said.

"Yeah," Mr. Carnivali said. "All this getting on and off the bus wears on you."

"Maybe you should sit the next one out," Al said. "Father, here, can check the list for you."

"That's a good idea," Mr. Carnivali said.

As the bus parked along the roadside at Little Roadtop, Mr. Carnivali reached over and handed his clipboard to Fr. Thomas and told him he wanted to sit this one out. "Sure thing," Fr. Thomas said, happy to be a more essential part of this stop where Colonel Joshua Chamberlain had saved the day for Colonel Meade's army as he had said in his homily. "Do you want some water?" the young priest asked and handed an unopened bottle across the aisle.

"Thanks," Mr. Carnivali said and loosened his tie.

As the pilgrims passed him on the way out of the bus, Mr. Carnivali told them that he was going to sit this one out and stay in the air conditioning.

Mr. Rawlings led the troupe up a little path to an open area at the crest of Little Roundtop where he could see all of the students and they could see behind and below him to the rise of the hill. When everyone was settled, he began his narration.

"So, the young Colonel Joshua Chamberlain was ordered to place the men of the Twentieth Maine along Little Roundtop to prevent the Confederate forces from flanking the Union position and collapsing the line," Mr. Rawlings explained. "He was told that reinforcements would be along shortly to support his regiment but, in any event, to hold this hilltop at all costs. Well, it wasn't long after they took their positions, that the first wave of Rebel soldiers came charging up the hill with rifles firing on the Union troops. The men of the Twentieth Maine held their ground and repelled the initial Confederate assault." Mr. Rawlings became more animated as he continued the story. "When the Southern soldiers regrouped, they charged up the hill, again and again, but each time they kept sweeping to their right," he used his hat to emphasize the troops' movement, "in an attempt to flank the Union forces. But, each time, they held the line. Colonel Chamberlain was anxiously waiting for the promised reinforcements because his men were running out of ammunition. He was afraid that they could not withstand another attack, so he ordered his men to fix bayonets to their rifles and led them in a bayonet charge down the hill to rout what was left of the Confederates and cause them to surrender. It was a bold and brilliant maneuver that military strategists have said saved the day at Little Roundtop and, possibly, kept the Confederate army from collapsing in on the Union forces along Seminary Ridge."

When he was finished, he could see that the students and chaperones were mesmerized by his vivid account of the bravery and quick thinking of Colonel Joshua Chamberlain. He noticed the tall Fr. Thomas smiling broadly behind the students.

A small, castle-like monument had been erected nearby in tribute to the men of the Twentieth Maine Regiment. Mr. Rawlings invited the students to go up into the two-story structure from which they could better survey the hillside where the Confederate soldiers made their advance. He told them to be back on the bus in fifteen minutes. The chaperones stayed close to the monument to be sure all of the students returned to the bus safely. As they walked back together, Fr. Thomas explained to Mr. Rawlings that he was delighted with his account of Little Roundtop as he had made mention of Colonel Chamberlain's heroics in his morning's homily at the Basilica.

The rest and water helped revive Mr. Carnivali. The driver had kept the bus idling with the air conditioning on to help refresh the principal. From his front seat, he welcomed the pilgrims as they boarded. He told Mr. Rawlings and Fr. Thomas that he had gotten his 'second wind' and was looking forward to the rest of the battlefield tour. The driver took the bus toward the final stretch of the tour along Seminary Ridge to the Union line facing Pickett's Charge. The ride took about ten minutes, enough time for Fr. Thomas to discuss with their guide the possibility of letting him address the pilgrims when they stopped at the statue of Fr. William Corby. Mr. Rawlings was only too happy to have the young priest take the microphone and explain Fr. Corby's role at the Battle of Gettysburg as it involved a Catholic sacrament, of which he was not too familiar, and, besides, his voice was beginning to horsen from the afternoon's narration. When they approached the statue of Fr. Corby, Mr. Rawlings instructed the driver to park along the roadside. Then, Fr. Thomas stood up and faced the pilgrims.

"If you look out of the windows on the right side of the bus," he began," you can see a large statue of a Catholic priest with his arm raised in blessing. That's a likeness of Fr. William Corby, the Catholic chaplain who served the Union soldiers during the three days of the battle. The statue commemorates Fr. Corby standing to give general absolution to the men of New York's Irish Brigade, with cannon balls exploding and bullets whizzing by, as they rushed to reinforce the Union troops defending Seminary Ridge. This brave, priestly action promised sacramental forgiveness to all the Catholic soldiers advancing into battle, and would prove to be a final act of mercy for the many who died that afternoon on the ridge." Fr. Thomas paused to let the significance of the sacramental action sink into the minds and memories of the students. "Fr. Corby's distinguished service at Gettysburg prepared him to become the President of the University of Notre Dame in Indiana when the war was over. If you look closely, you can see on the statue a representation of the stole a priest wears for confession. A replica of this statue stands near the small chapel built on the campus in memory of Fr. Corby's dedicated priestly service." The young priest returned to his seat, pleased that his morning's homily dovetailed perfectly with three of the leading, historical figures highlighted on the pilgrimage. He hoped that between his homily and what they learned throughout the day, the students would be inspired by the heroic lives of St. Elizabeth Ann Seton, Colonel Joshua Chamberlain, and Fr. William Corby.

As the bus continued along Seminary Ridge, the tour guide pointed out the monuments and cannons marking the various state brigades that manned the Union line.

He instructed the driver to pull over near the copse of trees that stood at the center of the North's position for the battle. Mr. Carnivali decided to sit this one out, too, rather than face the late afternoon sun. He handed the clipboard across the aisle to Fr. Thomas. "Do you mind?" he asked. Mr. Rawlings led their troupe to the highpoint in the Union line amidst the copse of trees, so that the pilgrims could view the wide field where the Confederate infantrymen made their fateful march.

"While several of the Confederate soldiers did make it to the copse," he began under the hot sun, "they were quickly killed or captured by the overwhelming Union presence. General Lee's calculated risk had failed to win the battle for the South as he had hoped. Historians point to this defeat as the first in a series of losses that would lead to the ultimate defeat of the South in the Civil War."

As they filed back onto the bus, Fr. Thomas checked off the students' names on the roster. "All present and accounted for, sir," he said when he handed the clipboard to Mr. Carnivali, in his best military imitation.

Once the bus started on the road, again, Mr. Rawlings held the microphone for one of the last times to prepare the pilgrims for the final stop of his battlefield tour. "We're heading to the Pennsylvania monument, the largest memorial on the battlefield," he said.

"If you walk around the building and ascend the stairs, you'll see the names of every Pennsylvania soldier who died at Gettysburg etched into the stone. The tourists usually like to take a group photograph on the dozen steps that lead into the monument. We'll expect you back on the bus in about twenty minutes," he said.

With youthful zeal, the eighth graders bounded out of the coach for this last exploration of the battlefield. The chaperones exited to keep an eye on the students; they had had a successful day helping Mr. Carnivali keep their group together. The students fanned out around and within the memorial, many of them reading and touching the engraved names of the fallen heroes.

Within a few minutes, Bobby Murray was leading a group of the boys and girls up the three flights of stairs to the top level of the monument. They waved to the less adventurous milling about on the grounds below. Inside the bus, Mr. Carnivali recalled how he used to race the students up the stairs to the top in his younger days, as there was no elevator in the building. After the students had sufficient time to explore the Pennsylvania Monument, Patty and Ralph Wiczneski gathered them on the wide steps in front of the memorial for a group picture. Most of the other chaperones were also prepared to take pictures on their cell phone cameras, especially those with eighth grade children.

One of the chaperones went to the bus to persuade Mr. Carnivali to join the group for the photograph. He felt sufficiently rested to make the trek off of the bus and up the stairs for the picture. He put on his sport coat and tightened his tie. Standing alongside the boys in the back row, he realized that some of them were already taller than him, though not taller than Fr. Thomas. After they had taken a few more photographs, they coaxed Mr. Rawlings to join the group for a couple more. Mr. Carnivali could feel the heat of the sun on his balding head and began to feel uncomfortable. He started to have some difficulty breathing. As the students disassembled to return to the bus, he felt lightheaded and leaned against a nearby pillar. When he felt a tightness in his chest, he quickly reached for the nitroglycerin tablets in his shirt pocket and clumsily placed one under his tongue to dissolve. For a moment, he thought he was going to black out. He prayed a silent "Hail, Mary,' as the pill began to take effect.

"Are you okay?" Fr. Thomas asked as he neared the aging principal, and held his arm in support.

"Just a little dizzy," he said as he loosened his tie and took off his sport coat. "Could you hold this, please;" he handed his coat to the priest. "Just give me a minute or two. It should pass." He took a few deep breaths, while steadying himself against the pillar. "Help me down the steps."

Fr. Thomas gave him his strong arm to hold onto as they descended. One of the chaperones, a nurse, approached them when they reached the bottom of the stairs. "How are you feeling?" she asked, watching his breathing and observing the color in his face. Mr. Carnivali remembered that Mrs. Tate was a nurse.

"It's passing," he said. "I took a nitroglycerin pill and it's easing the pressure;" he put his hand to his chest. "My doctor says I have a slight heart murmur. I should be fine when I get on the bus in the air conditioning."

Fr. Thomas and the nurse escorted him to the bus, careful to help him up the steps. He seemed to regain his composure when he sat down in the cool coach. The nurse found a bottle of water for him to sip. She held his wrist to check his blood pressure on her watch.

All of the students and most of the chaperones were unaware that Mr. Carnivali had an incident on the stairs in front of the monument. When he was sure the principal was relaxed and out of any immediate danger, Fr. Thomas asked the driver to wait a few minutes while he checked off the students' names. He walked through the length of the bus, with the clipboard roster with him. The nurse sat in the seat next to Mr. Carnivali to keep an eye on her patient.

"You gave us a scare, Pete," Al said to his friend.

"For a moment, I thought I was crossing over to the other side," Peter said. "My wife's going to give me hell."

Mr. Rawlings told the driver to go back to the Visitors Center where he parked his car. As he was preparing to leave with his black bag, Mr. Carnivali handed him a folded fifty dollar bill and thanked him for the excellent tour on behalf of the pilgrims. When the bus stopped and he took the microphone to say 'good-bye,' a spontaneous round of applause expressed the pilgrims' appreciation for his expertise. "If I don't see you, enjoy your retirement, Pete," he said to Mr. Carnivali and shook his hand. With a tip of his hat, Mr. Rawlings departed the bus.

"Our last stop is in town at the Jenny Wade House," Mr. Carnivali said to the driver.

"That's the one on Steinwehr Avenue," the driver said. "I know where that's at."

After several more minutes, the driver double-parked the coach in front of the Jenny Wade House to unload the pilgrims. The house bore a bronze plaque near the door with the date of its erection: 1842. Mr. Carnivali was feeling better, now, and encouraged Fr. Thomas and Mrs. Tate, the nurse, to go inside and see how the battle impacted the women and children left in their homes when their husbands and fathers went off to war. He assured them that the worst had passed and that he would be fine on the bus with the air conditioning. He did not want to go into the small house with its cramped hallways and narrow staircases filled with his pilgrims. When everyone was off of the bus, the driver drove a little farther down the street to park along the curb and wait for his passengers. Mr. Carnivali explained to him that they would take about half-an-hour to tour the three- story home and basement.

For several minutes, the principal closed his eyes and tried to decompress, finding some rest in the cool coach. The trip was more grueling than he had expected. Alice had warned him that it might be. I'll call her in a few minutes, he thought, wondering how he would tell her about the incident. When he felt sufficiently rested and ready to call his wife, he took his cell phone out of his coat pocket and hit the speed dial button for their land line. It rang a couple of times before she picked it up.

"It's me," he said. "We're at our last stop before we go to General Pickett's Buffet for supper…Things went well… Al Rawlings was our tour guide for the battlefield… You remember—he was the guy who carried the black medicine bag with the cannonball and other stuff… He's still going strong… I'm fine…I got a little dizzy in the hot sun when we were taking the group photograph at the end… Yeah, you're right dear, I should've worn a hat… No, I'm okay… I just sat out this stop to avoid the tight quarters in the Jenny Wade House… It gets a little close… I stayed in the air conditioned bus with the driver… The kids should be out shortly… We should be home in a couple of hours … I can't wait to see you and tell you all about it when I get home… Good-bye, Alice… Bye, bye." He put his cell phone away and closed his eyes, again. He was breathing more easily, now. He took a few sips of water. I'll tell her the whole story when I get home and she can see that I'm okay, he thought.

The driver stepped out of the bus to wave to his passengers as they began trickling out of the house. While they were in the house, the rumor had spread that Mr. Carnivali was sick. They walked the half-block to where the bus was idling. Fr. Thomas checked off the names as they boarded. The last one to get on was Bobby Murray. When he saw Mr. Carnivali sitting in the front seat, alone, he bent down and gave him a hug. "Thank you, sir," the boy said to his principal and then hurried down the aisle.

"What was that about?" Fr. Thomas asked as he came in after Bobby.

"He's not as tough as he lets on," Mr. Carnivali said. "He just needs a chance to to be good."

"Well, folks," the bus driver said into the microphone. "Our last stop is at General Pickett's Buffet for supper. It's been a real joy taking you around today. You're as fine a group of young people as I have ever brought to Gettysburg."

Again, a round of spontaneous applause expressed the pilgrims' appreciation for their bus driver. Mr. Carnivali had an envelope of cash ready for his tip when they got back to Harrisburg.

Mr. Carnivali leaned across the aisle to speak to Fr. Thomas. "After supper, when we're on the highway, will you lead us in the rosary, Father?"

"I was hoping you'd ask," Fr. Thomas said.

Mr. Carnivali leaned back in his comfortable seat, grateful to God for His goodness and mercy, and the many blessings of the day.

THE END

Blue Grass

First Day

"There's no such thing as a Bigfoot, Bobby," Edward said to his son in exasperation. "That's just your grandfather talking."

"He said Daniel Boone shot one while he was hunting for deer," Bobby insisted.

"He showed us the story in the newspaper," Barbara came to her big brother's defense.

"Yeah, he saw one himself when he was a boy fishing on the Chillicothe River," Bobby said.

"There's no pictures, no evidence." Edward turned around to face his children sitting in the seat behind him and Susan on the bus. "Just that copy of an old wrinkled up newspaper article from the early 1800's. I grew up with this stuff; most of it's apocryphal." Edward had grown up in Berks County, Pennsylvania, 2 where the Boones had lived with the other Quaker families before the young Daniel sought his fame and fortune on the Kentucky frontier. He had heard all the legends since he was Bobby's age.

"But he told us what it looked like," Bobby countered under his father's withering glare.

Then the motor coach bumped over the expansion joint in the middle of the bridge, jostling the forty passengers as they left Cincinnati and crossed the Ohio River into Kentucky. The slight bump seemed to settle the argument about Daniel Boone and early American cryptozoology.

"It's just a story," Susan soothed her husband. "He told us the same ones when we were kids." Susan had been waiting and wondering when the ongoing conflict between Edward and her children was going to erupt. The children had admirably restrained themselves in front of the other pilgrims and with Fr. Steven sitting across the aisle from them. Only once since they left Pittsburgh had the tension revealed itself: during that brief lunch stop at the Kentucky Fried Chicken outside of Columbus when, as they were getting off of the bus, Bobby and Barbara suggested that their grandfather had lost the recipe for that famous chicken to the Colonel in a poker game on a steamship making its way down the Ohio River. Then, Susan had tried to suppress her chuckle so as not to further exasperate her husband. But, now, it was as if crossing the Ohio River into Kentucky signaled the end of the uneasy truce and the potential for an all out confrontation, with Edward on the side of reason, history and science, and her two children advocating for their deceased grandfather's tall tales, myths and folklore more than facts. It's going to be a long three days, she thought.

As the tour bus rumbled along Interstate 71, Fr. Steven started to give the pilgrims a brief instruction about the origins of horseracing in the ancient world on the bus' scratchy speaker system, stretching the spiral cord on the microphone from the 3 dashboard to his front seat behind the driver. But the young priest hadn't gotten more than a few sentences into his history of horseracing sermon when he was drowned out by loud and contentious voices emanating from the middle of the bus, where the men and women members of St. Mary's choir were arguing about what they wanted to do tomorrow during the hour, or so, of downtime in the late afternoon.

Susan could hear the strained pitch of their harsh voices, with some of the men wanting to tour the Louisville Slugger Plant, where baseball bats had been manufactured for over a hundred years, and more women pressing for a shopping trip to the commercial district in downtown Louisville to see the season's selection of derby bonnets, among other fashionable apparel. She offered to calm them down for Fr. Steven, since she was the bus captain, but the zealous, young priest thought it was his ministerial duty to mediate the divisive dispute that threatened to divide his pilgrim flock along gender lines. So, he walked down the aisle to settle the rancorous debate, eventually resorting to the expedient explanation that they probably wouldn't have that much time tomorrow anyhow, let alone "to choose between hats and bats," as he put it succinctly. And while the choir members quieted momentarily, neither side seemed satisfied with their priest's negotiated settlement, as he swayed back up the aisle toward Susan, trying to keep his balance as the bus swerved on the highway.

Susan advised Fr. Steven to skip the history lesson, trusting that the tour guide would probably cover some of that at Churchill Downs or, if not, expecting that they could see it for themselves at the adjacent Kentucky Derby Museum which was already on their itinerary. She deftly tried to deflect the conflict for her children, explaining that the ladies just wanted to go shopping while the men wanted to see the place where they made the baseball bats they used since they were little boys Bobby's age. She hoped her explanation would satisfy her children and not increase the tensions that had already risen between them and their father. Lord knows, she thought, don't want to throw more fuel on that fire.

When they got to Churchill Downs in Louisville, their bus driver turned off of Central Avenue and into the spacious parking lot, following the wide driveway that led to the entrance. Susan and Edward were the first ones off of the bus, with their kids in tow. The driver handed Ed a step stool to place at the open door of the bus to facilitate the pilgrims' exit. Fr. Steven went ahead to secure their group's tour time as they were a little late. As they got off the bus, Edward offered his hand to the women and few children, and the older men if they would take it. Susan appreciated the way her husband volunteered to assist her in her role as bus captain. "Thank you, kindly, young man," one of the older more wobbley ladies said to Edward as he eased her exit.

"Just go straight to the entrance there," Susan said, pointing to the glass doors. "Fr. Steven will meet us inside."

It was a beautiful summer day, and after several hours on the bus Susan could see how relieved the people were to finally get somewhere. She thought the long bus ride partially explained the crankiness of the choir.

Once everyone was off of the bus and in the vestibule of the museum, they still had to wait for the dozen, or so, who had to use the restrooms. Trying to keep forty people together was a real challenge; somebody was always going off on their own, or lagging behind the group, or trying to buy something when it was time to move on. It was Susan's job to herd the stray sheep as Fr. Steven led the way. Once everyone was gathered, Fr. Steven introduced their tour guide who proceeded to direct them to the museum's entrance where they would begin their self-guided tour. "Meet me righ'cher at 3 pm sharp," Linus Albright said, "and I'll teacha a thing or two about horse racin' in Kentucky."

So, the forty pilgrims and Fr. Steven made their way through the turnstiles. The Derby Museum was filled with saddles and riding crops, horseshoes and jockeys' jersies, photographs and placards illustrating the origin and development of this great American race, the first of what eventually would become known as the Triple Crown, once the Preakness and the Belmont Stakes were added to the spring racing cycle. Edward walked behind Bobby as they made their way along the displays, stopping to read a few, while little Barbara held her mother's hand as they strolled by the artifacts, seemingly more interested in sharing an intimate moment together than the history of horseracing in Kentucky.

Susan was startled by a life-sized model of one of the famous thoroughbreds, relieved that it wasn't the work of a taxidermist but merely a synthetic replica. She tried to keep an eye on the dozens of pilgrims milling through the museum's maze of exhibitions, watching for those who might dally, here and there, and drift away from the group. Then she felt Barbara's kiss on the back of her hand and stooped down to give her a hug and a kiss on her cheek.

"I love you, Mommy," Barbara said to her mother, the child obviously happy to have her to herself for a while.

"I love you, honey," Susan said and hugged her again.

It took about half-an-hour for the pilgrims to make their way through the museum and reconvene in the vestibule around Fr. Steven. Counting heads, Susan suspected that they had lost a few to the restrooms and a couple more to the gift shop with its display of derby bonnets. She asked Ed to check the men's room as she and Barbara went to the ladies' room to gather the stray sheep. After several minutes, everyone had returned and the tour guide began his spiel.

"Well, I understand that y'all from Pittsburgh," Linus Albright began. "The Gateway to the West it was called back in the day when Kentucky was the western frontier of these United States—but back then, a couple hundred years ago, Kentucky weren't even a state at all, just the western-most county of Virginia where fast horses were the necessary trade and travel of the pioneers who risked life and limb to settle these unexplored Shawnee lands."

Standing in front of their parents, Bobby and Barbara looked at each other with amazement, their mouths open in wonder because this middle-aged man could have been a younger version of their grandfather for the way and rhythm of his talk. Susan noted her children's fixed stares; Linus Albright had them mesmerized.

"Now, careful where you step," Mr. Albright cautioned the pilgrims as he led them outside to the stables and track. "The horses came through this way for their mornin' trot."

The half-dozen children in the group, including Bobby and Barbara, let out a collective and unintelligible sound of disgust.

"Look up yonder along the edge of the grandstand and y'all see those big medallions with the names of the horses and the year they won the Derby over these past one-hundred-twenty-five years that this great race has drawn folks from far and wide to bet on the fastest and noblest four-legged mammals the good Lord ever created," Albright raised his lanky arm and waxed almost theological as he led the group to the race track.

"Where's Seabiscuit?" Bobby blurted out, unable to contain himself as he recalled his grandfather's stories about the little Kentucky thoroughbred who was so fast 'his hooves nary touched the earth.'

"Now, there's a boy knows somethin' about horseracin'," Linus said and smiled at Bobby. "But no matter how hard we search, we won't find a medallion for Seabiscuit because, though he was born and bred in Kentucky, he never ran in the Derby. He made his name beating War Admiral in the most famous match race in the history of American horse-racing."

"If memory serves," he continued with a sly smile, "the original owners were from your Pittsburgh: the

Carnegie-Phipps families. But they gave up on that wonder horse when he started out 0-17 and sold him to some Californian. With a new diet, training regimen and fresh jockey, they turned that little stallion into the winningest horse of 1938, retiring from competition a couple years later having won nearly a half- million dollars in prize money—the most ever back then."

Bobby and Barbara turned around to glance at their father.

Susan recalled her father's talking about the legendary racehorse when she was a little girl and how he took the whole family to Louisville to see the movie starring Shirley Temple and Barry Fitzgerald at Churchill Downs for the fiftieth anniversary of his stunning victory at Pimlico over War Admiral, the Triple Crown winner the year before. She found herself nodding with her children as Mr. Albright confirmed her father's stories about the legendary 'people's horse'.

"Story goes that President Franklin Delano Roosevelt himself was late for a news conference because he was listening to that match race between Seabiscuit and War Admiral on the radio along with forty million other horse-lovin' Americans," Mr. Albright said in a climax to his dramatic telling of the Seabiscuit legend that concluded with the leader of the free world. "Let's make our way to the track." He led the group to the edge of the race track, to an open space where the horses were led in and out before and after the race. He regaled the pilgrims with more stories about the famous politicians, movie stars and musicians who came each year to witness the most celebrated horse race on the continent, as he pointed out the various sections of the grandstand and the planned expansion of Churchill Downs the following year. After answering a few more questions about capacity and cost, Linus led them back the same way they came, reminding them to be careful where they stepped.

In the museum lobby, Susan nudged Fr. Steven, who then slipped a twenty-dollar bill into Mr. Albright's hand.

"Good children you got here, ma'am," he said to Susan as he tussled Bobby's hair. "Right smart, too."

Susan, Edward and their children moved to the rear of the group as the pilgrims followed Fr. Steven through the large doors and onto their waiting bus. Susan had to encourage some of the ladies to complete their transactions in the gift shop, including some of the choir members who were determined to purchase a derby bonnet. Finally, everyone was boarded.

As they drove to the Bardstown Motel about an hour south of Louisville, where they would be staying for the next couple of days, Susan was thinking about her father, Hiram, and the formative impression he had left on her children the past few years, ever since her mother, Rebecca, had died and they had moved him to Pittsburgh to live with them. Many a night he had put his grandchildren to sleep with the same tall tales she had heard when she was a girl in Kentucky: tales of Daniel Boone and the Shawnee Indians on the frontier, apocryphal stories of legendary horseraces, accounts of government revenuers searching the woods beyond Boonesborough for the hidden distilleries that kept many of their neighbors going, yarns such as how the recipe for whiskey was brought to Kentucky by the great Boone himself, and, the most preposterous of all, she recalled, the disputed burial site of the quixotic frontiersman: Missouri, where he died or Kentucky, where he belonged.

"What are you smiling about?" Edward said to Susan, interrupting her reverie.

"Happy to be home, hunh?"

Susan nodded to his satisfaction and leaned against him. She was thinking about how her children, Bobby, ten, and Barbara, eight, were young enough to believe the folk tales their grandfather told them when he had tucked them into bed, yet old enough to realize that they would never hear his gravelly voice again, nor fall asleep in his arms on the rocking chair in their living room. So, now, several months after he had died, the kids were still mourning his death, crestfallen at the mention of his name or the remnant aroma of his pipe tobacco lingering about their home.

"Folks," Gus, the driver, broke the relative quiet of the bus. "There's some kind of slow down ahead, an accident or breakdown or something. Nothing to be worried about. We'll be past it in a few minutes," he said as he slowed down their motor coach to just a few miles per hour.

Susan saw the Kentucky State Police cars, lights flashing, flanking what appeared to be a double tractor trailer that had jackknifed off of the highway and onto the shoulder of the road. Once they had driven through the congestion, Susan recalled why and how she arranged for their pilgrimage in the first place. She had intuited, with maternal prescience, that the only way she could relieve her children's grief was to visit the land of those stories and verify the 'truth' of their grandfather's version of Kentucky's fabled history. So, a couple of months after her father's death, she began a subtle campaign with the newly ordained priest at Saint Mary's to take a parish pilgrimage to the Abbey of Gethsemeni in Kentucky, where Fr. Thomas Merton had lived, written and directed souls. She knew that Fr. Steven had written his 'tesina' in Rome on Merton's Seven Story Mountain and would be anxious to visit his former Cistercian community at Gethsemeni. She had persuaded Fr. Steven that they could also tour historic Bardstown, the oldest Catholic diocese west of the Allegheny Mountains. And if the parishioners did a little sightseeing along the way, all the better, she had thought, for her children's sake and in memory of her father and the place she had grown up as a little girl and teenager. It hadn't taken much to convince Fr. Steven to let her organize the pilgrimage, so here they were in Kentucky several months later.

At the motel, the Baudry family and Fr. Steven got off of the bus first, with Susan getting the room keys at the front desk to distribute to the pilgrims while the porters got the luggage from the bay beneath the bus.

"Give them about an hour, Father," Susan said to Fr. Steven. "To get settled, rest and freshen up."

"We'll meet here at six-thirty," the young priest announced, allowing for the inevitable stragglers. "Our reservation is for seven o'clock."

The bus ride to the restaurant was only several blocks away, so the delay while Thelma Ostrowski found her lost room key, in her shopping bag as it turned out, still enabled the pilgrims to arrive on time for supper. The Bardstown Inn was situated below the town's Civil War Museum, which unfortunately, was closed in the evening. Susan could tell from the way Bobby and Barbara asked her how far away the restaurant was that her children, and most of the pilgrims, for that matter, were hungry for a good meal after the long day on the bus and at Churchill Downs.

The pilgrims had preordered their entrée when they registered for the trip: prime rib, pork chops or barbecued chicken, with the potatoes, vegetables and salad on the buffet. The polite waitresses brought the plated meats to the two long wooden tables, simply asking the people what they had ordered, and then directing them to the buffet for the sweet potatoes and mixed vegetables, the tossed salad, cornbread and butter. Pitchers of water and sweet tea were already on the tables along with glasses and utensils. Susan prodded Fr. Steven to offer a quick grace before the hungry pilgrims got into the buffet line. The young priest, pleased that the first day of his first parish pilgrimage had gone well, offered a familiar prayer, blessing their food and fellowship and giving thanks to the heavenly Father for His providential care.

Waiting for the other table of hungry pilgrims to go first, Edward used the lull to begin discussing Kentucky's neutral stance in the Civil War to those within earshot.

Susan noticed her children's eyes glaze over in boredom so she gently kicked her husband beneath the table, trying to prevent another eruption before they ate.

The pilgrims moved through the buffet line quickly, each passing through on one side or the other. Susan helped Bobby and Edward assisted little Barbara with the vegetables, potatoes and salad. Once seated and settled, the pilgrims enjoyed the plentiful food and abundant fellowship at the close of the first day of their journey. With the people sitting in clusters of families, friends or couples, Susan appreciated the lively table conversation while they enjoyed the delicious food— her barbecued chicken especially tasty, the crunchy texture of the cornbread, the brewed tea sweet and refreshing. She helped her daughter cut her chicken thigh.

"The meal's included in the cost of the trip," Susan said to Edward. "But if you want a drink, it's extra."

"I'm not driving," Edward said, looking for the waitress to order an after dinner drink to top off his prime rib supper.

As the people finished their meals, the waitresses came around to pick up their plates and bowls and ask if they wanted dessert: chocolate cake, apple pie or butter pecan ice cream. Susan ordered the cake, the kids ice cream, Fr. Steven the pie.

"I'm going to skip dessert," Edward said as the waitress took his plate. "But I could go for a scotch and soda."

"You mean bourbon, doncha?" the tall waitress said. "Ice?"

Edward hesitated a moment to determine if she was joking. He felt another kick under the table and glanced at Susan. "Yeah," he capitulated. "Maker's Mark with some ice."

"They're nothing if not loyal," Susan said to her husband. "It's an industry around these parts—feeds a lot of families."

After a couple of enjoyable hours at table, the pilgrims were ready to retire.

Susan directed her sleepy children to get on the bus, while she and Edward waited until everyone was accounted for: forty men, women and children, including them and the priest.

Back at the motel, the weary pilgrims made their way to their respective rooms on the first two floors, with the Baudry's room off of the vestibule and a little way down the hall from the breakfast nook.

As they alternated the use of the lone bathroom, Susan suggested to Edward that she would sleep with Barbara and Bobby could sleep with him. She knew her little girl would enjoy being close to her mother in this strange motel room. Once everyone was washed and changed into their nightgowns or pajamas, Edward led them in the Our Father, the Hail Mary, and the Glory Be. A chorus of 'good nights' closed the day. When Susan reached over her already dozing daughter to shut off the light on the night stand between the beds, she saw the harmonica that Barbara was holding in her little hand close to her face. She got the faintest whiff of her father's Kentucky leaf tobacco still evident on his hand-held wind instrument months after his death. Snuggling around her daughter, Susan finally let herself relax into a peaceful sleep on the firm motel mattress and plush pillow. As she drifted off to sleep, she could hear her husband's slight, rhythmic snore as her harried mind coalesced memories from the day's excursion with random reminicences of her young life in Kentucky.

Then, she and Edward were on their summer break, approaching her family home near Boonesboro to tell her parents about the engagement: her mother, Rebecca, in the doorway with the screen door opened; her father, Hiram Sutton, sitting on the porch in his rocking chair like some potentate puffing on his pipe, until they were on the steps and he stood up, pointing that pipe at Edward, and declared: "So, this is the Frenchie wants to take my baby girl outta Kentucky!" And she, waking from the dream 13 with her feeble defense on her lips: "But he hardly speaks French." Barbara stirred for a moment with her mother's whisper. Then, Susan calmed herself in the dark and tightened her arm around her little girl, trying to go back to sleep, the memory of her mother and father fresh and dear. Before she dozed off, she remembered how her father had eventually accepted her marrying a Catholic of French descent, and later, even her inevitable conversion to Catholicism, but he had not been so forgiving about her leaving Kentucky, as had most of her siblings. As she closed her eyes, she could almost hear her father's incredulous question: "How could you ever want to leave Kentucky?" as if she was abandoning some ancient center of Western Civilization like Rome or Paris or London.

Second Day

Susan was the first to wake and then, Edward, shortly after she began preparIng herself in the bathroom for the day ahead, both of them letting their children sleep as long as possible. As she tried to quietly wash her face, brush her teeth and brush her long, auburn hair, Susan was becoming excited for the day's itinerary. She recalled the only other pilgrimage her family had taken, to the St. Anthony Chapel on the North Side of Pittsburgh a couple of years earlier for the Year of Mercy. The little chapel on Troy Hill had been designated an official pilgrimage destination with a plenary indulgence granted to visitors to venerate the second largest collection of saints' relics in the world after the Vatican's own collection in Rome. After her quick shower, while she applied her makeup and lipstick, she remembered the life-sized stations of the cross and the beautiful paintings and tapestries adorning the walls. She recalled Bobby and Barbara's excited report to their grandfather when they got home later that afternoon, putting him in the untenable position of minimizing the sanctified charm of Catholicism while clinging to his own enchantment with his legendary and native Kentucky. "Bones and beads," she could almost hear him muttering under his breath, not wanting to scandalize his impressionable and Catholic grandchildren whom he loved dearly.

"I'll get the kids up while you're getting ready," she said to Edward as they eased past each other at the bathroom door. "How did you sleep?"

"Terribly. Now I know why he's so good at soccer—he must've kicked me a dozen times," Edward said.

"How can you look so beautiful at dawn?" He placed his hands on her waist above her thin blue bathrobe.

"Nevermind, mister," Susan coyly feigned resistance, thrilled that his desire for her was always simmering beneath even their most brief exchanges after a dozen years of marriage.

As she tried to wake the children, she recalled her father's lament: "Of course you had to fall in love with the last living Frenchman in Berks County, and a Catholic to boot." She could barely restrain her giggle over the memory of her father's feigned indignation. Sitting on the bed, she held her little girl asleep in her arms. The harmonica lay aside the pillow. She wondered how many times she had said to Edward over the past few years: "They're just stories...his way of passing on something of him- self to the kids," to ease the tension between her husband and her father before it escalated into a protracted campaign of distrust and stealth like the frontier skirmishes between the Shawnee and the early settlers of Kentucky. She knew that neither man could refuse her subtle mediation. She laid Barbara's head back down on the pillow, her little fingers near his harmonica.

Then Susan nudged her son. "Time to get up Bobby," she whispered near his face. The boy rolled away from his mother's persistent voice. "You're next to use the bathroom after your Dad."

Susan utilized her children's reluctance to rise as an opportunity to change into the dark slacks and floral blouse she had selected for the day's excursion.

"You look great, honey," Edward said when he came out of the bathroom.

Susan smiled with the compliment. "Can you get Bobby up?" she said.

"Barbara's still asleep."

Edward dutifully pulled the covers off of his son, who had been stirring since his mother's whispered entreaty. "C'mon, Robert; time to get up," Edward insisted. Bobby slowly rolled out of bed and padded to the bathroom. Edward used the lull to put on his shirt and pants, his socks and shoes.

When Susan finally got Barbara out of bed, the little girl had her grandfather's harmonica in her grasp, again. Susan recalled her father's reluctance to move in with them to Pittsburgh after his wife died. He had finally agreed to come only because Edward had grown up in the same Pennsylvania county in which Daniel Boone was born and raised and had attended Daniel Boone High School and so, he figured, "He can't be all bad, even for a French Catholic, if his people rubbed elbows with the Boones." Susan smiled with the memory of her father's spurious reasoning as she began to lay out Barbara's bright, yellow outfit for the day.

When Bobby came out of the bathroom Susan asked him if he had brushed his teeth to which the boy nodded without looking at her. "Well, then," she said. "After breakfast." Then she led Barbara into the bathroom to help her get ready. Before she closed the door, she heard her husband barking orders to Bobby not to lay down on the bed again and to get dressed for breakfast.

"So, what's it going to be: pancakes or waffles?" Edward asked the kids in a way that was more a challenge than a question as they walked down the hallway.

"Pancakes," Bobby said.

"Waffles," Barbara countered and squeezed her mother's hand.

"They have both," Susan said and gave her husband a glance for stirring up the breakfast drama that always got the children going, with the men, including her father, wanting the pancakes and her and Barbara preferring the lighter, crispy waffles. It was one of the few domestic matters that had put her husband and her father on the same side. "I read the motel's breakfast menu when I was planning the trip."

Everyone seemed satisfied with Susan's calming appeasement. She had that maternal way of negotiating the family tensions, especially while her father lived with them, a kind of intuitive sixth sense that enabled her to keep the domestic tranquility at all cost, without requiring a humiliating capitulation from anyone. She just knew how to coax peace in all directions, like it was some innate wisdom given her at birth.

The Baudry's met some of the other pilgrims at the breakfast nook. Some of their troupe had already eaten. Susan helped Barbara ladle the batter onto the hot waffle iron and close the lid. They sat down at a table of four, with Edward's and Bobby's plates stacked high with pancakes and sausages. "Coffee's good," Edward said to Susan as he passed her the creamers.

"Father Steven," Susan said between bites of her waffle. "We board at 9 am for the Bardstown tour and then Mass at St. Joseph Cathedral." Fr. Steven nodded in acknowledgement as he finished his coffee and danish at a nearby table with some of the parishioners.

Susan and Barbara enjoyed their waffles and bacon with a kind of feminine empathy that made each forkful seem even more tasty because they were enjoying the waffles together that Edward and Bobby weren't. The maple syrup and butter were rich and delicious over their crunchy, warm waffles.

After breakfast, the pilgrims got on the motor coach with Luella, the local tour guide. Susan was happy to relinguish leadership for a while and leaned against her husband while Luella pointed out some of the Civil War buildings, the railroad station and the quaint town square whose storefronts recently had been given new colorful facades. Susan had been in Bardstown before, both before and after she became Catholic, so she was familiar with the local history and landmarks.

She closed her eyes, her belly full, and recalled how she and Edward had met at college during her second year in Pittsburgh. He was studying robotics at the prestigious Carnegie-Mellon University while she was a student at the exclusive School of Nursing at the University of Pittsburgh with the whole UPMC network of hospitals just about guaranteeing her work in the tri-state area after graduation. They had literally bumped Into each other at a rock concert on Flagstaff Hill, the grassy hillside that sprawled between the two campuses. He was a junior and she was a sophomore, they began meeting for coffee on Craig Street, the little commercial district between CMU and Pitt. Within a few months, they both realized they were falling in love and were talking or texting, throughout the day, sharing the mundane details of their classes and laboratories with a fresh excitement that suggested their growing affection. After trying a variety of exotic cuisine on Craig Street, Edward and Susan had settled on Ali Baba's as their weekend favorite, with its middle-eastern lamb shish-ka-bob, delicious mint salad and savory rice with pine nuts, their usual meal. It became their romantic place to be alone together and play out their courtship at a quiet table in the corner of the popular restaurant. Usually, they split the baklava for dessert. Those intimate suppers shaped their future lives together when, at last, they would marry after they both had finished at their respective universities and found work in Pittsburgh: he at the CMU Robotics Institute and she at the new UPMC Children's Hospital, both in the Lawrenceville neighborhood, where they would eventually buy a house. They were engaged for a couple of years before they got married. Edward, from a small family, was hesitant to take on the full duties of family life until he was financially secure, while Susan, the youngest of six siblings, was anxious to begin her own family. "You asleep?" Edward whispered and gave Susan a little squeeze around her shoulder.

"Just dozing," she said, snuggling a little closer to him.

"Alright folks," Luella said. "We're coming up to St. Joseph Cathedral where Father, here, will be havin' Mass for ya'll."

Susan thanked the middle-aged former mayor of Bardstown for her informative morning's tour, prompting the pilgrims to clap their appreciation. Then she stood in the aisle and tapped the microphone to check if it was still on. "Now, remember," she said. "When we get inside, find a seat toward the front. Fr. Steven will begin at ten sharp. Don't start wandering around the church. After Mass, we've arranged to have one of the cathedral docents give us a little talk about this beautiful Basilica of St. Joseph."

"Bobby," Susan said to her son away from the microphone. "You get off with Fr. Steven and help him prepare for Mass—you'll be serving, too."

As soon as the tour bus parked in the front lot, Fr. Steven, notebook in hand, and Bobby got out and hurried up the stairs. Edward and Susan helped the others disembark, directing them up the stone stairway and through the large wooden columns that marked the entrance to the Basilica.

Once inside, Susan and Edward met the docent who helped them usher the forty pilgrims to the front pews of the Church. Susan noticed that the altar candles were already lit and the other appointments for the liturgy were in place. Within a few minutes, a gentle bell signaled the beginning of Mass, with Bobby in black cassock and white surplice leading Fr. Steven in green vestments to the front of the altar where they genuflected in reverence. Holding Edward's hand in the front pew, Susan recalled the many times she went with him to Mass at Saint Paul Cathedral or the Pittsburgh Oratory near their campuses on Sunday evenings while they were courting. Edward was a devout Catholic, which she had always admired about him even though she had been raised a Kentuckian more than anything else. Still, she had found the solemn prayers and chanted hymns, the ancient rituals and sacramental supper, appealing on some intuitive level. Even now, after she had been a Catholic for more than a decade, something about the Mass always enveloped her sensibilities and soothed her heart. The paintings and pillars that lined the walls and aisles of this formidable Basilica filled her eyes with their beauty and symmetry.

Following the scripture readings, Fr. Steven's homily was a carefully prepared, scripted history of the pioneering effort of the Church to establish the Diocese of Bardstown in the early nineteenth century and build the first Catholic cathedral west of the Alleghenies. Though the docent would repeat most of the dates and names, Fr. Steven provided his pilgrim flock with an historical account of the Maryland catholics who migrated to Kentucky for a couple of decades before the arrival of the French Bishop Benedict Joseph Flaget in 1811, just before the War of 1812, Britain's last attempt to colonize the fledgling nation. Fr. Steven spoke respectfully of Bishop Flaget's determination to build a majestic cathedral in the western frontier of the United States using the materials from the surrounding wilderness and the labor of the locals. He explained how Bishop Flaget built the Cathedral of St. Joseph to replace the smaller St. Thomas Church that originally served the Catholic community in Bardstown. "Consecrated in 1819," Fr. Steven concluded, "the exterior of this beautiful cathedral would be completed a few years later."

When it came time for communion, Susan and Edward led little Barbara to Fr. Steven standing at the edge of the sanctuary. Their daughter displayed the same innocent faith that had characterized her initial reception of the Lord only a year ago. Susan's eyes watered momentarily with the recollection of Barbara in her frilly white dress, veil, socks and patent leather shoes, that May morning at St. Mary's. Her daughter's First Holy Communion, with all the ceremony and pageantry, had somehow fulfilled Susan's own desire to have had such a day as a child. "Amen," Susan said as she rose from her bow and Fr. Steven placed the consecrated host on her tongue. After Mass, the tall docent's talk was more about the art and architecture of the Basilica than its history, seeing that Fr. Steven had already given his parishioners that lesson. "The architect and builder was John Rodgers of Baltimore," she began, standing in front of the pilgrims still seated in the pews. "The paintings and sculptures that beautify this historic edifice were gifts donated by European royalty, including the Kings of France and Sicily, among others."

"Where did they get the big pillars on the outside and inside of the church?" Mr. Covelli asked the docent.

"The columns were hewn and lathed from native poplar trees," she answered. "And the bricks were baked right here in the old Bardstown kiln."

"Why is it called a Proto-Cathedral?" Joan Miller asked, looking up from her brochure.

"With this region growing in the early nineteenth century," the docent explained, "the diocese was moved north to Louisville in 1841, about forty miles from here. Then, St. Joseph became a parish church with the honorific title of 'proto-cathedral,' or first Cathedral."

Susan was glad there were no more questions. Shortly after Fr. Steven and Bobby returned to their group, she suggested that they should be on their way, as they had a full day ahead of them.

"Well, thanks for visiting our two-hundred-year-old house of Catholic worship in Kentucky," the docent said. "Oh, and one more thing. In two-thousand and one, Pope John Paul II, of happy memory, conferred the title of a Minor Basilica to St. Joseph Proto-Cathedral because of its unique historical and aesthetic features. We're also designated as a national landmark by the U.S. Department of the Interior." As the pilgrims followed Susan and Edward to the doors of the church, another docent handed some of them a copy of the thin brochure that included still another version of the storied history of the Bardstown basilica, with a listing of the paintings and sculptures and their respective donors.

Once the forty pilgrims were back on the motor coach and the driver pulled out of the parking lot, the petite Luella spoke with Gus about the couple of stops they would make before going south to the Abbey of Gethsemeni in New Haven.

Within a few miles, Bobby and Barbara started up again about their grandfather, asking their mother why

Grandpap never went to church with them except on Christmas and Easter.

"Well," Susan hesitated. "He believed in his own way. He was a good man and loved us very much." She recalled her parents taking the whole family to the little chapel by the creek whenever the preacher passed through their village once every month, or so. But, she remembered, it seemed to be more out of a sense of Sunday duty than personal devotion. During his few years with them in Pittsburgh, she knew better than to push him on matters of religion. "He wasn't Catholic like us," she explained.

The children accepted their mother's explanation and, then, became distracted by the large black buildings on both sides of the interstate highway.

"What are those?" Barbara asked Luella, who was sitting with Fr. Steven in the seat behind the driver, as the bus whizzed by several more of the dark monoliths dominating the landscape.

"Folks," Luella began into the microphone. "If you look out your windows on either side, you'll see those big black warehouses along the highway and back aways." She paused a moment for the pilgrims to get a good look at the vast fields of storage facilities. "Those are where they keep the barrels of bourbon while they age. You can see that there are no windows and they're painted black to keep out the sunlight. They aren't the prettiest things but the demand for Kentucky bourbon has grown so much across the country, and even world-wide, that these acres of warehouses have sprung up all over the countryside the past thirty years, or so."

"How long does the bourbon have to ferment?" Mr. Ninehouser asked Luella from a few rows behind her.

"Five years," she said, "to make smooth bourbon whiskey. Some longer."

"Grandpap said they were like transformers," Bobby said to Barbara. Hiram had concocted that fabrication while watching Bobby playing with his transformers changing trucks into robots. "He never trusted them. He said some of them were secret silos that could change into FBI robots to find the last tobacco patches and whiskey stills in Kentucky."

"Robert," Edward said as he turned around, over-hearing his son repeating one of their grandfather's tall tales verbatim. "Don't fill her head with that stuff. They're just warehouses where the bourbon ferments." Edward always thought that his father-in- law's bour-bon-robot government conspiracy theory was a swipe at his life's work at the Institute.

"Big tobacco companies bought up most of the fam-ily-owned patches in the eighties and nineties when I was serving on Council," Luella chimed in overhearing Bobby's explanation to Barbara. "The feds were trying to regulate tobacco sales back then. There's just a few of them left, now."

"See," Bobby said trying to defend his grandfather's preposterous theory. "The government was surprising free Kentuckians."

"Surpressing, Bobby," Susan corrected her son, suppressing her laughter at his parroting of her father's yarn. "Kentucky's changed a lot since I grew up here. Sometimes your Pap just made up some stories to explain the changes."

"How can you tell the true ones from the made up ones, Mommy?" little Barbara asked her mother.

"Good question, honey," Edward said and gently nudged his wife.

"Folks," Luella addressed the pilgrims on the microphone, sparing Susan from trying to make a convoluted hypothesis that would satisfy her children, her husband and the memory of her father. "We have to make a stop up here to pick up our boxed lunches. We'll get off the bus for a few minutes at Lincoln Park to eat our lunch."

Once the burly bus driver, Gus, parked near the nondescript cafeteria building, he, Luella, Edward and Fr. Steven got off to get the food for the forty hungry pilgrims.

In a few minutes, they came out of the Bardstown Co-op carrying large boxes with their food and drinks. Gus opened one of the bay doors and slid the boxes inside next to some remnant luggage and a few cases of water.

On their drive to the park, Susan overheard Luella explain to Fr. Steven that she had helped form the community cafeteria to serve the poor in town and employ some of those who were slow or had some disability. She could tell that the former mayor was proud of her civic contribution.

The park was a short, pleasant ride to the edge of town on this beautiful June day. The sky was clear and blue; the sun bright and warm. When they got off of the bus, Luella and Susan led the pilgrims to the picnic benches within the large pavilion. Gus, Ed and Fr. Steven placed the boxes of food and drink on one of the empty tables.

Like the buffet last night, the people walked by and chose their lunch sandwich, the boxes marked ham or turkey, and took a can of cold soda or a bottle of water. Fr. Steven led the thanksgiving prayer over their impromptu picnic, before the people enjoyed their boxed lunch, which also included fruit, bags of chips or pretzels, cole slaw, utensils and a cookie. Some of the pilgrims traded their fruit or snacks in a spirit of frontier bartering.

A few bees buzzed around them as they ate their lunch amid quiet chatter, many of them facing the field beyond their shelter. Light blue puffs of something seemed to hover above the grass that covered the field.

"Kentucky blue grass," Luella stood up to address the pilgrims, noticing their curious gaze. "A kind of weed that grows above the green blades giving the fields around these parts that soft blue canopy. It'll be gone in a few weeks."

Bobby and Barbara looked at each other in amazement while they ate their cookies, recalling their grandfather's stories about the "blue grass of Kentucky—the only place on earth where God wanted his grass to be the color of the sky." Susan smiled when she noticed her children in awe of this unique regional feature and remembered her father's proud insistence on just another reason why "Kentucky was like heaven on earth."

"See," Bobby said to his father sitting across from him on the picnic bench. "Blue grass like Grandpap said."

Edward just shook his head and kept eating, not wanting to get into it with his petulant son in front of the other pilgrims at the table.

When the pilgrims finished their lunch, Gus, Edward, Luella and Susan gathered the waste into a couple of large plastic bags and put them in the garbage cans near the bathrooms, where the bees buzzed around the recepticals. Nearby, a few men smoked cigarettes.

Once they were all back on the bus, Luella and Gus discussed the best route to go south to the Abbey of Gethsemeni in New Haven. Fr. Steven listened intently to their brief discussion because the Trappist Monastery was the personal highlight of the pilgrimage for the young priest.

"Folks," Luella said to the pilgrims as the bus pulled out of the parking lot. "We have a bit of a ride, so just sit back and relax. Susan, here, will be giving out some postcards I got showing the monks praying at mealtime. They don't say too much," Luella continued. "They mostly pray."

Susan handed out the postcards depicting about a dozen Cistercian monks in their white and black habits standing at table. She moved deftly down the aisle, making sure that each pilgrim got one in anticipation of their next stop. She knew that Fr. Steven was excited about visiting the monastery where Fr. Merton had lived and worked. She was happy to help facilitate this part of their journey because it was the principal reason that Fr. Steven encouraged her to organize this parish pilgrimage, though he had suspected she might have her own reasons to return to her home state, too.

With their bellies full, the pilgrims seemed content to let the bus driver worry about getting to the next leg of their day's excursion. When Susan returned to her front seat with Edward, she noticed Barbara beginning to nod off to sleep, her eyes drooping. Once on the highway, she knew that the vibration of the bus would enable both of her children to get some rest before the day's full itinerary. Edward's eyes were closed, too. Quiet for a moment, Susan had second thoughts about their decision not to take the children with them to Kentucky last year for her father's burial next to her mother in the small cemetery at Boonesboro. It was during the school year and she and Edward weren't sure how the children, especially the younger Barbara, would handle their first experience of a family death. She was hoping this trip would be a way of making up for that lost occasion for them to say good-bye to the grandfather they loved so dearly and the grandmother they barely knew. And from what she had seen and heard from her children, so far, it seemed to be working as they encountered the Kentucky alive in their grand-pap's stories.

The ride to Gethsemeni took them off of the main highway and through the rolling hills of the Kentucky pastures and farmland. It was on this uneventful part of their pilgrimage, with her husband and children dozing and the passengers relatively quiet, that Susan felt the deepest yearning for her homeland. It had only taken a couple of days, but the Kentucky that was in her blood, her heart and memory, rose to the surface with each breath that filled her lungs, soothing her eyes and ears with familiarity. She remembered running barefoot across fields like these with her sisters and brothers after wading through the shallow stream near their family's home. For half an hour, she was lost in those recollections of her carefree Kentucky childhood and teenage years, as the bus carried the pilgrims to the New Haven monastery.

Luella directed Gus to park the bus near the edge of the small lot, closest to the monastery chapel. In deference to the monks gathering for their mid-day prayer, Luella reminded the pilgrims to keep silence. She told them they could use the restrooms before going into the chapel, where they would be seated in the pews behind a wooden partition. Fr. Steven, carrying his black valise, was the first of them to enter the chapel and settle into a pew for prayer; a few of the locals were already in the pews. Susan put her finger to her mouth to quiet little Barbara when she began to ask her mother some question. "Hush, now, baby," she whispered close to her ear. It took several minutes for all the pilgrims to use the facilities and fill up the pews. More than once, Luella had to remind them not to talk as she ushered them to their seats. One by one, the monks in white habits and long black scapulars entered the chapel and took their seats in the choir stalls facing each other.

In respect for their vow of silence their places were not close together. Once the dozen, or so, were settled in their places, a soft wooden knock signaled the entrance of the abbot to start their midday prayer, only one of several gatherings for prayer in the daily life of these strict Cistercians.

"God, come to my assistance," one of the monks intoned the chant.

"Lord make haste to help me," the others responded in an ethereal tone.

For the pilgrims, keeping silence while the monks chanted the psalms and antiphons, read the brief scripture verses, concluded their prayer and walked out of the chapel, was a new experience. So used to socializing after Mass, Luella had to remind a few of them to be quiet, again, until they were outside.

"They take a vow of silence," Susan explained to her children as they walked to the gift shop.

"Maybe something you kids should try," Edward teased his son and daughter.

"It's a sign of their total devotion to God," Susan continued. "To prayer and work."

"They don't even talk during meals," Luella explained to some of the reticent pilgrims as they approached the gift shop. "One of the monks reads aloud while the others eat."

The tinkle of the bell as the door opened seemed to signal that it was safe to start talking again and so the chatter resumed as the forty pilgrims packed the gift shop, browsing through books, religious objects, miscellaneous souvenirs and the famous fudge and fruitcakes.

As the woman at the counter began to ring up their purchases, a couple of the pilgrims asked about the volunteers who assisted the monks.

"There's about a dozen of us who help out in the gift shop or the office," she happily replied. "Others just come for prayer."

It didn't take long for the line to back up with most every couple purchasing some fudge and many the fruitcakes. Rosaries, medals, books written by Merton, crucifixes, small statues of favorite saints and hand-crafted icons, plaques and leather belts were the most popular items among the flurry of shoppers. A taller woman joined her colleague to help bag the gifts and move the line more quickly.

When Fr. Steven, holding a small plastic holy water bottle, reached the counter, he asked the volunteer if he could speak to the Prior, the monk who ran the day-to-day operation of the monastery. "I have something to give him for the Abbey."

"Oh," she said, familiar with securing the occasional donation for the monks.

"I'll let him know, but it could take a few minutes."

It took about twenty minutes for the pilgrims to complete their shopping. Susan bought some mugs of various colors for her family with the image of the mona- stery on them as a practical momento of their trip for when they got back to Pittsburgh. "He'll be right down," the taller woman said to Fr. Steven, who was near the counter as she hung up the phone.

The pilgrims were milling about the property outside that was open to the public, holding their plastic gift bags. They could see the cemetery less than a hundred yards away where the graves of the monks were marked by simple black crosses.

Fr. Steven met the Prior at the door of the gift shop. He had carried his black valise with him during the afternoon's visit.

"Thanks for coming," Fr. Steven said as he shook hands with the balding Prior.

"I'm the one that wrote you last month about giving a copy of my 'tesina' to the monastery library. I've had it bound." He reached into his valise and pulled out the scholarly work he had written for his licentiate degree in Rome. "It's entitled 'Thomas Merton's Seven Story Mountain and the Catholic Mystical Tradition'."

"Thank you, Father Steven," the Prior said as he accepted the two-hundred page typescript. "Did you sign it?"

"No," he hesitated. "I didn't think to."

"C'mon," the Prior said. Fr. Steven followed him into the gift shop. "Lilly, can I have a pen?" the Prior said, laying open the text on the countertop to the title page. He handed the pen to Fr. Steven. "Here, above your name."

"The comparison includes St. John of the Cross, St. Teresa of Avilla and St. Therese of Lisieux, among others," Fr. Steven muttered as he carefully signed his name. "This is exciting for me—I've been anticipating this trip for months."

"Keep it," the Prior said when Fr. Steven extended the pen back to him.

"We'll put this with the other books written about Brother Thomas' published work," the Prior said as they left the gift shop with the bell tinkling. "There's quite a few."

"Thank you," Fr Steven said, shaking hands again with the Prior.

"No, thank you for your dedicated interest in the gifts of our community," the Prior said. "Thanks, too, for bringing your people to pray with us. I trust they found some things to take home with them to Pittsburgh. The fudge has a little bourbon in it—that's the secret ingredient," the Prior said and gave a little wink and a slight smile to Fr. Steven as he turned away.

Fr. Steven returned with the others as they boarded the bus. Susan could see that he was delighted to give a copy of his thesis to the Abbey of Gethsemeni where Merton had lived and worked. She was happy for him, happy that the pilgrimage had fulfilled a personal connection for their shy young priest. Lord knows, she thought, it's fulfilling mine, too.

Once everyone was settled on the bus, gift bags in hand, Susan leaned across the aisle. She offered some fudge to Fr. Steven, who was still holding the pen, and to Luella and set a piece on a napkin on Gus' dashboard. There was enough for her family, too.

Some of the other pilgrims were also opening their boxes of fudge, enjoying the rich, sweet chocolate with the secret ingredient.

After she had eaten her piece of fudge, Luella got on the microphone to tell the pilgrims about their next stop. "We're headed to the Maker's Mark Bourbon Distillery next. So, sit back and enjoy your fudge as we go from one kind of Kentucky spirit to another," she joked, with most of the pilgrims chuckling at her tour guide humor.

The ride on the two-lane winding road took the pilgrims across more pastures and farmland. Because of the turns and hills, Gus had to drive more slowly, so Susan took the opportunity to put in a short dvd about the life of Stephen Foster in anticipation of their attendance at 'The Stephen Foster' show that evening at the outdoor amphitheater in My Old Kentucky Home State Park outside of Bardstown.

The dvd was about half an hour long and covered the highlights of America's first and most popular minstrel, including his life in Pittsburgh. She had borrowed it for the trip from the Carnegie Library at the Stephen Foster Center just a couple of blocks from where they bought their home on Fisk Street in Lawrenceville. Susan and her children had previewed the dvd a few days earlier and Bobby and Barbara had learned some of the lyrics and melodies of his most popular songs. Their proximity to the center was another reason her father cited for tolerating the move from Kentucky to Pittsburgh.

"It can't be all bad if Stephen Foster lived here," Hiram opined when he finally moved in with them.

Between the delicious fudge and the entertaining dvd, the pilgrims were subdued for the most part, except when some of the members of the choir chimed in with a few bars of one or another of Stephen Foster's original songs from the dvd that most everyone knew. Susan leaned back over her seat to help her children sing along with the choir. Even Ed and Fr. Steven joined the impromptu sing-along. Before they knew it, the motor coach was pulling into the large parking lot of the Maker's Mark Distillery complex, its buildings highlighted in red like the bourbon bottle itself.

"Here we are, folks," Luella announced to the pilgrims. "Leave your bags on the bus—Gus'll lock it up for us. Who knows, you might be coming back with some more souvenirs."

Luella was the first to get off the bus to meet the lady who would walk them through the distillery. The tall, attractive woman, in jeans and a bright blue blouse, greeted the shorter Luella with a friendly smile and handshake; they had done this a few times before. "This is the church group from Pittsburgh," Luella said as the pilgrims slowly emerged from the bus..

For a few minutes, the woman waited for the people to gather near her before they entered the distillery. "My name is Mae, like the month," she began. "And I've been giving these tours for the past few years. My

110

brother works here, too, on the loading dock, among other things. Y'all picked a beautiful week for your trip." Once the rest of the people were out of the bus and Susan herded them around Mae, she began her recitation in a pleasant, rhythmic voice. "So, y'all from Pittsburgh," she said. "A church group I can see from Father, here. Well, the growth of bourbon makin' in these parts is almost a miracle itself. During my lifetime, the production has increased to every corner of these United States and most developed countries in the world. In fact, Japan is one of the biggest importers of Kentucky bourbon in the whole world."

"C'mon, now," Mae beckoned with a wave of her arm toward two couples approaching the group. "You can join us; we're just getting started." The young couples stood behind the Pittsburgh pilgrims.

"I'll be takin' y'all through the oldest part of our distillery; it's been remodeled and fancied up some for the tours," Mae said. "If you look between and beyond these buildings here, you'll see some big quanset huts like they use in the military," she continued, pointing to the few aluminum buildings visible to some of the group.

"They were put up years ago to accommodate the growing demand. Today, most of our bourbon is distilled in those facilities, not in the buildings you'll be seeing. But the process and machinery is basically the same. Follow me, please."

As Fr. Steven, Luella and the others followed Mae into the large building, Susan, Edward and their children moved to the rear of the group. It took a few minutes to position the forty pilgrims and the few latecomers inside.

"Okay, now," Mae said in her clear strong voice. "Can everyone hear me?" she asked, watching for their nods. "These two large vats are filled with the mash, water, sugar, and other ingredients that ferments for thirty days, to begin the process of making whiskey. D'y'll know what makes bourbon bourbon?"

"Corn," Mr. Ninehouser said.

"That's right. Of the grains that go into the mash, fifty-one percent, and no less, must be corn to produce that sweet taste and rich color of bourbon that distinguishes it from other types of whiskey," Mae said. "The story goes that settlers from your Pennsylvania brought the recipe for rye whiskey here, maybe even Daniel Boone himself, and that the genius of the locals tweaked that recipe with the corn that grew plentifully around here. And so, we have Kentucky bourbon."

When she mentioned Daniel Boone, Bobby and Barbara perked up and strained to listen to the rest of her speech.

"How many gallons of mash in each of those vats?" Mr. Ninehouser asked.

"Enough to keep the group of us in good spirits 'til the next Derby, and then some," Mae said, drawing a chuckle from the pilgrims. She began to lead them to the next chamber but stopped short of the door. "The plexiglass sealing the vat room is there for our protection. The fermentation process renders carbon monoxide gas which if you get a strong whiff can knock you out. The guys who work in there stirring the mash have to wear safety masks despite the exhaust fans."

The next room was filled with copper pipes and tubing which Edward found especially interesting. Mae waited for the whole group to assemble, again. "Here's where the distillation takes place," Mae said. "Through a series of steps of heating and cooling, the mash is filtered and refined into its raw form. I don't know too much about the science of it; the bourbon master usually does this part but he's already done for the day—he starts at dawn," she explained. "There's some placards on the wall there if y'all are interested." Some of the pilgrims read the explanation on the placards near the tubing and kettles. Edward studied each one carefully.

"Be careful, now," Mae said as she led the group down a stairway that led to a long, dark hall. Mae waited for everyone to enter the hallway. "Here's the storage room where the raw bourbon is placed in oak casks to age for five years. Look up; the barrels are stacked to the ceiling."

"They saw the hundreds of warehouses along the highway this morning," Luella said to Mae.

"All of these barrels will eventually rotate their way to the warehouses you already saw on the highway," Mae said. "Five years aging in those warehouses and the bourbon's ready to be bottled. I might add that our empty oak barrels are eventually sold to the distilleries in Scotland where they reuse them to age their famous scotch whiskies."

Mae led the group out of the storage area, up a few steps and across a little patio into another building where the labels were affixed to the empty bottles along a rattling conveyer belt that snaked its way around the room. She took her time, as she was accustomed to wait for the stragglers to catch up.

"The conveyor belt and labeling machine are primitive forerunners of the robotics technology we develop at work," Edward said to Bobby and Barbara, who were more focused on the train of clear bourbon bottles passing through on the other side with new labels affixed to each. As the people walked out of the bottling room, Mae handed each of them a sample label as a souvenir. As they moved into the next room, Susan noted the way Doloris Thomson had been holding her husband's arm throughout the tour, seemingly more for intimacy than balance.

When everyone was gathered, Mae started again. "Now, here's where the labeled bottles are filled precisely with the aged bourbon from the oak barrels and capped to complete the process." Another conveyor belt carried the bottles under the spouts and to a machine that twisted the cap onto the glass threading on the neck of the bottle. The tour had taken about forty-five minutes, or so, and many of the older pilgrims were anticipating a break to rest their legs.

Just in time, Mae directed the group to another room. "Everybody find a seat, please," she instructed the forty plus people to be seated around a large u-shaped table, already prepared with five thimble-full tastes of various types of Maker's Mark bourbon on trays at each place setting. "Except any of you children —you step back here with me and Luella for a glass of Dr. Pepper."

As Mae invited the pilgrims to taste the different types of bourbon, most common to most expensive, she briefly gave the names and explained the differences in taste and cost. "Now, try to remember your favorite before we go into the gift shop in case you want to make a purchase."

Some of the wives only tasted one or two of the bourbons offered and then slid their tray to their husbands, who seemed happy to help them finish the samples. "Now, don't get up too fast," Mae said. "We have time for you to browse through the gift shop and pick up some souvenirs to take home to Pittsburgh."

Susan thanked Mae for her informative tour of the distillery and prompted some of the nearby pilgrims to clap their appreciation. She nudged Fr. Steven again, and he slid a twenty-dollar bill into Mae's hand as he thanked her personally.

As the last of the pilgrims finished the bourbon tasting and got off of the stools, Mae led the others down a hall, across a courtyard and into the remodeled gift shop. It had been recently enlarged to accommodate the increase in tour groups. There were clerks at the registers and circulating around the store, handing out small shopping bags with the Maker's Mark brand printed in red. The people needed little encourage- ment to buy various bottles of bourbon, coffee mugs, caps, tee shirts, coasters and miscellaneous novelties. After several minutes, the two registers were ringing up the sales, with both lines a half-dozen deep.

"What's she doing up there?" Josette Taylor asked one of the roving clerks and pointed to the raised platform where a woman in an apron was dipping bottles into a slowly spinning pot.

"She's sealing the bourbon bottles with our signature red wax," the clerk explained. "Do you want to try it?"

"My bottle is already sealed," Josette said as she lifted the bottle out of her shopping bag.

"We can switch it," the clerk said and took an unsealed bottle of bourbon from a nearby shelf and traded with Josette. "Go ahead. Just step up. She'll show you how."

"It's easy," the woman said as she took a bottle, turned it upside down and twirled it in the hot red wax.

"Just the top of the neck—a couple of inches," she said. When she turned the bottle right side up the wax immediately congealed in a bright and random collar on and below the cap.

"We'll let it dry a moment," the woman said and set her bottle on the nearby table. "C'mon, you try it, now."

Josette, who led the quilting group at the parish, adroitly turned her bottle into the hot red wax with a twist of her wrist. A small group of pilgrims had gathered to watch one of their own try her hand at the sealing process. When she lifted her bottle out of the pot, she had successfully formed an attractive wax seal around the neck similar to the clerk's.

That was all it took—someone to try it. Within minutes, several of the pilgrims had lined up at the platform to seal their own bottle of Kentucky bourbon. While they waited near the doors of the gift shop, Susan and Luella were talking about how much time they had to get back to the motel before supper and the evening show. They had more than enough time but not enough to go to Louisville for the "hats and bats." Susan explained to Luella yesterday's conflict on the bus. Before the people began boarding, Luella gathered them in the courtyard for Mae one last time. "Well, it's been a true pleasure taking you on our tour this afternoon," Mae began. "I want to thank y'all for your kind attention, especially the children, who learned more

117

about bourbon making than they should know." The pilgrims clapped in appreciation of Mae's informative and thirst-quenching guided tour.

"So, Luella tells me you've already been to Churchill Downs," she said. "Well, with Father's indulgence, that means you've experienced most of the 'Kentucky Trinity': horseracin', bourbon and tobacco—though these days not so many folks are smoking, let alone chewing. Have a safe trip the rest of the way." Mae waved goodbye until the last of them, Susan and Edward, got on the motor coach.

On the bus, Bobby and Barbara were talking excitedly by the time their parents finally took their seats.

"I'm telling you, Barbie," Bobby insisted. "That's what Pap used to say. Tell her, Mom, about the three things," Bobby appealed to Susan for support.

"It's just an old saying," Susan said over the back of her seat, conscious that Edward, let alone Fr. Steven, might not be so happy with her confirming the familiar, if slightly irreverent, Kentucky aphorism to her children. "We all heard it growing up." The phrase sparked recent memories of her father putting some bourbon on his fingertip when the children had a toothache or were cutting new teeth, and of how he gently rubbed their gums to dull the pain. She recalled how her parents applied that Kentucky home remedy to her and her siblings when they were children, too. The ride back to the motel would take about forty-five minutes, or so.

Gus was in no hurry as they had plenty of time before supper and the evening show at the amphitheater. He stayed close to the speed limit, not taking any risks on the winding two-lane road. The passengers were chatting about the day's adventures or looking over their purchases at the monastery and distillery. He had been to both places several times with other tour groups. The summer ride through the grassy fields and farms was relaxing enough for him and the pilgrims, some of whom even dozed off, the bourbon still on their breath. Behind him, in his sideview mirror, he saw a pickup truck gaining speed, seemingly determined to pass the bus. As they approached a slight hill, Gus realized that he couldn't see much more than a hundred yards ahead. He tried to wave to the driver of the pickup truck to slow down but he only kept coming faster, crossing into the other lane. Not wanting to risk an accident, Gus slowed down the bus and eased onto the shoulder of the road to let the truck overtake them and swerve back into their lane just before he reached the summit of the hill.

"Hambone!" Gus muttered as the young man in the pickup sped quickly ahead of them on the downside of the hill.

Though she was unsure of what happened, Susan, overheard Gus' frustration and repeated the word, 'Hambone,' under her breath. It was the word her father used when he was frustrated with someone's stu-

119

pidity. Occasionally, he used harsher words around her brothers, that she had sometimes overheard, more vulgar and coarse. But around her and her sisters and mother, he used words and phrases that were rough but humorous, and she recalled that he never took the Lord's name in vain. 'Hambone,' she whispered again, relishing her father's deference to their feminine sensibilities, realizing his paternal restraint, recalling the little smirk he would make to laugh away their surprise when they were within earshot of his perturbed mutterings. 'Hambone' she said to herself, again.

When they got back to their motel in Bardstown, Susan took the microphone to thank Luella for her help and familiarity with the local sites. Everyone clapped. When Fr. Steven shook her hand to thank her, he remembered to give Luella something extra to supplement her tourguide fee.

"Y'all've been a joy to be with, today," she said into the microphone. "Enjoy the show tonight."

Susan gave Luella a friendly hug before she got off of the bus. She appreciated her help in leading the way for the pilgrims during this second day of their trip.

"You have enough time to freshen up, drop off your souvenirs, and be back on the bus by five o'clock," Susan said into the microphone. "We're having a picnic supper at the state park at five-thirty and the show begins at seven—it's all on your itinerary." With this fourth unloading of the forty pilgrims, some of the older people were complaining about their aches and pains, their backs and legs, as they entered the motel. Susan walked up and down the center aisle of the bus to be sure that everyone had remembered to take their gift bags.

Like the rest of the wayfarers, Susan, Edward, Bobby and Barbara were anxious to get to their room, freshen up and rest for a while. Susan, and many of the other women in their group, also planned to change their outfits for the evening's supper and musical performance.

"So, why is our library named after Stephen Foster?" Barbara asked her father as he rested on the bed.

"He was originally from Pittsburgh," Edward said, repeating the explanation he had told his children a few days ago in preparation for the trip. "There's a statue of him in Oakland where Mommy and I went to college."

"That's where you met, Mommy," Barbara said to her mother as she recalled the stories Susan told her.

"Prettiest girl on either campus," Edward said and got up to hug his wife who had changed into her colorful flowered dress. "Still is."

"Oh, Ed," Susan feigned disinterest in his show of affection. "Don't wrinkle my dress."

The children chuckled at their parents' flirtatiousness; they had witnessed their playfulness many times before.

"Time to go," Susan said as she picked up her purse from the dresser. She had to be a little early to make sure the other pilgrims were on board the bus by five o'clock.

At the bus, Susan checked off the names as the couples and the others boarded. "Is Thelma with you, ladies?" she said to the last few getting on the bus. "She's the last one," Susan said, checking her watch and the list of pilgrims with their room numbers. "Tell Father I went to get Thelma," she said to Gladys. As Susan started down the motel hallway, she saw Thelma walking toward her in her recognizable slow gait.

"I'm coming," Thelma said. When she met Susan in the vestibule, she pleaded her case. "I couldn't find my nicer pair of shoes."

Once everyone was on the bus, Susan explained that the state park and amphitheater were on the outskirts of town, not even fifteen minutes away. "I'll give you your tickets when we get there," she said as Gus pulled out of the parking lot. "We have the dinner-theater package, so you've already paid for everything," she reminded the pilgrims.

Traveling together, sharing meals and accommodations, experiencing new places and interesting people, Susan could see a bond forming among the people, most of whom were from St. Mary's, with several others from neighboring churches or relatives and friends of the core parish group. Things were working out as she had hoped: Fr. Steven was thrilled to present the copy of his 'tesina' to the Abbey at Gethsemeni; the pilgrims were getting along well enough and managing the challenges of travel; and her children were getting a glimpse of her storied Kentucky home that her father had brought to life in their imaginations with his tall tales and fabled fabrications. And for Susan, the pilgrimage was a kind of tribute, reviving the memory of her larger-than-life father who died last year in her home in Pittsburgh, states away from his beloved Kentucky.

When they arrived at My Old Kentucky Home State Park, Gus was directed to drop off his passengers near the main pavilion and then park the bus in the back of the large lot. Susan asked Ed to hand out the tickets to each of the pilgrims as they got off the bus, while she went ahead to find out where their group would be seated for supper. The savory aroma of the grilled meats wafted through the evening air as the people followed Susan to the large picnic shelter reserved for their Pittsburgh group. They were seated near the buffet line and close enough to see the cooks flipping racks of ribs, hamburgers and pieces of barbecued chicken on the grills. This was the first week of the summer season for "The Stephen Foster Story" and there were already a couple of hundred people in the shelter and the amphitheater on this warm summer night, with hundreds more expected for the evening's musical show. Within a few minutes, Susan was told to lead her pilgrims to the long buffet where the wait staff would help serve the supper. No one bothered to ask the St. Mary's group for their tickets as their reservations were made months in advance and they were the only out-of-state pilgrimage group that night.

After the full day of touring, the pilgrims enjoyed the delicious barbecue supper, which included potato salad, baked beans, a tossed salad, fresh cornbread and butter to complement the grilled meats and plenty of paper napkins for those eating the ribs, with lemonade, sweet tea and water the choice of beverages. Eating outside on this fair June evening only enhanced their appetites, so most of them had room for the apple, berry or cherry pie that was served for desert with ice cream and coffee. Susan cut Barbara's hamburger in half so the little girl could handle it more easily. The lively chatter at their tables suggested to Susan that despite their full itinerary that day, the pilgrims were anxious to see and hear the show. She left her family at the table so she could secure forty good seats for her group. She was pleased that the ushers had already set aside a section of seats to accommodate the out-of-town guests.

Susan made sure that everyone was seated by six-forty-five so that they had ample time to get settled, use the facilities and review the program. The stage was large with a painted background of lush trees and bushes and a beautiful stately home. The amphitheater held a few hundred people for the night's show.

The hour-and-a-half performance was thoroughly charming. From the moment the actor playing Stephen

Foster came on stage strumming his banjo in top hat, long plaid coat and red bow tie, the audience was captivated. The projected sound in the outside amphitheater was excellent. The nearly forty singers and dancers in the troupe were dressed in nineteenth century garb, with the women especially attractive in their colorful hooped skirts, bonnets and ribbons. The story traced Stephen Foster's origins in Pittsburgh to his meteoric rise in popularity as the father of American music. They sang many of his favorite original compositions, danced in their period costumes and acted out the dramatic moments of the minstrel's life. The audience, including Fr. Steven's pilgrims, could not restrain themselves from chiming in on the most familiar songs, like 'Beautiful Dreamer,' 'Camptown Races,' 'My Old Kentucky Home,' and, for the finale, 'Oh! Susanna'. The music was still familiar to this regional audience almost two-hundred years after the songs had first made an impact on American popular culture. Susan, of course, knew all the words by heart since she was a little girl. Except for when little Barbara asked her mother 'if you wore dresses like that when you lived in Kentucky,' Susan's children were fascinated by the lively singing, the twirling dancers and the audience's response to the engaging performance under the Kentucky starlight on this pleasant June night.

On the bus ride back to their motel, some of the choir members were singing those favorite folk ballads, further evidence of how the composer's musical genius was still popular. When they got to their motel room, Susan and Barbara started dancing like the women in the show, singing a few bars of those catchy songs. Barbara took out her grandfather's harmonica and tried to play along with her mother's pleasant singing. Edward told Susan that he and Bobby were going to take a walk around the building to see the stars, again, before they went to bed, but he really just wanted some time alone with his son. Without missing a beat, Susan waved her acknowledgement and kept twirling around the cramped room with her gleeful daughter.

When they got to the rear of the building, Edward suggested to Bobby that they sit down at the table and chairs on the small patch of grass at the edge of the parking lot.

"Did you enjoy the show?" Edward asked his son.

"Yeah," Bobby said. "It was fun."

"You and Barbara knew some of the lyrics," Edward said.

"Mom taught us," Bobby said.

"Are you still carrying around Pap's pipe?" Edward asked.

"How did you –," Bobby began to defend himself.

"Don't worry," Edward interrupted his son. "Let me see it."

Reluctantly, Bobby took the pipe out of his front pants pocket and gave it to his father.

Edward took out a small leather pouch from his own pocket and some matches. He proceeded to fill his father-in-law's pipe with the dry tobacco and struck a match. He held the lit match above the bowl and inhaled slightly. He exhaled a few puffs of smoke.

"I didn't know you smoked, Dad," Bobby said.

"I don't," Edward said. "This is the last of your grandfather's Kentucky leaf tobacco and it seems wrong to let it go to waste—even if it's a little dry."

"It smells like the house," Bobby said as tears misted his eyes.

Edward drew on the pipe until he was sure the tobacco was hot and burning.

"Do you want to try it?"

"Am I allowed?" Bobby asked. "We won't get arrested will we?"

"No—just don't tell your mother," Edward chuckled at his son's caution.

"Just take a couple puffs and taste the smoke in your mouth and then blow it out; don't inhale it into your lungs."

Bobby took the pipe from his father and raised it to his lips. He mimicked his father's draw on the smoking pipe and managed a few puffs of the tobacco without coughing.

"That's enough," Edward said and took the pipe from his son. He smoked it for a few more minutes until the dry tobacco was burned out in the bowl. Edward tapped the residue ash out of the pipe and onto the grass. Then he got up.

"Let's hit the sack," he said to Bobby and put his arm around his son as they walked around the building. He could see the glistening tears in Bobby's eyes. "Let's keep this our little secret between you, me and your grandfather, 'young man,' " he said, addressing his son the way Hiram always did. "Brush your teeth before you kiss your mother 'goodnight.'"

"Okay, Dad," Bobby said, happy to have the warm pipe back in his pocket. Thankful to have a father who understood.

Third Day

Susan woke up to find Barbara snuggling into bed with her, still holding Hiram's harmonica near her face. She felt secure with Edward's arm around her and his body keeping her warm beneath the bedsheet. She could smell the faintest scent of her father's tobacco on the harmonica in Barbara's hand. Bobby's kicking finally got to her, she thought as she pressed her daughter closer to her, placing her arm around her little back. She did not want to get up just yet and closed her eyes to avoid seeing the digital clock on the nightstand. When she opened her eyes a few minutes later, she saw the glowing green numbers: 6:25 am. They were scheduled to board the bus at eight-thirty on this final day of the pilgrimage. Her family would have enough time to wash, get dressed, pack and get some breakfast. In her husband's arms, holding her little girl, with her son barely an arm's length away, Susan could have stayed in Kentucky for another week; it seemed like a dream come true. Slowly, she got out of bed to begin her family's routine of waking.

After all of the pilgrims had readied themselves, packed their suitcases and had some breakfast, Susan, Edward and Fr. Steven helped Gus put the many suitcases in the bay beneath the idling bus. Susan dutifully checked her list to make sure everyone was on board by going down the aisle and eyeballing each person, most of whose names she knew by now. She couldn't leave anyone behind on the last day. "I'm here," Thelma Ostrowski said when Susan got to her seat near the back of the bus.

"Early, for once," her roommate, Gladys, teased her friend.

"Everyone is present and accounted for," Susan said to Gus when she returned to her seat next to Edward.

Gus took the microphone to speak with his passengers on their last day.

"Folks, I've enjoyed being your driver these past couple of days. I'm looking forward to our final day together," he said. "You've been kind and courteous and I just want to say that I've had as much fun as you've had. Thanks for letting me be a part of your pilgrimage."

Susan and Edward began clapping but the pilgrims needed little prompting to express their appreciation for their driver's steady hand at the wheel.

Once they were driving on the interstate and toward Lexington, the next big town before they would turn off to see the Ark replica, Gus got on the microphone, again. "Folks, the locals call this stretch of highway the 'Blue Grass Parkway' for obvious reasons. Like we saw yesterday at that Lincoln Park, the fields on either side of the road are covered with that puffy blue weed that grows above the grass like little cotton balls. Some places it's more prominent than others but you can see patches of blue most everywhere along this highway in the summer."

"Blue grass," Barbara said to herself as she looked out of her window, recalling her grandfather's description of Kentucky as 'heaven on earth,' as he put it. Within the hour, the tour bus passed through the horse ranches that sprawled across these rolling hills all the way to Lexington. The pilgrims were engrossed watching the white, black, brown, tan and calico colored horses trotting in the fields, eating the sweet grass and, occasionally, chasing each other playfully. If Western Kentucky was famous for horse racing, Eastern Kentucky was renowned for breeding the stallions, mares and colts that might compete for glory in future races. The beautiful horses prancing amidst the blue grass of the meadows and hills reminded Susan of how much she truly loved Kentucky as their motor coach continued through the acres of ranches approaching Lexington on Interstate 71. Shortly after Gus turned south on Interstate 75, toward Williamstown, he took the microphone again and told the pilgrims to start looking for the massive replica of Noah's Ark. On this clear, sunny day, it would be visible to them from half-a-mile away.

As soon as the huge structure was in view, Fr. Steven began instructing his flock about the builder's decision to place the vessel on the approaching hilltop to suggest the biblical ark's settling on Mount Ararat after the forty days of flooding. Never one to miss an opportunity to teach, Fr. Steven told the pilgrims that the project had taken a hundred skilled Amish carpenters more than six years to construct it according to the exact biblical specifications found in the Book of Genesis. "It's about five-hundred feet long and fifty feet high," he concluded.

Susan took the microphone for a moment to inform the pilgrims that all of the lumber for the exterior of the ark was purchased from the Snavely Forest Products Company in West Mifflin, a suburb of Pittsburgh. She knew the local connection would be interesting to the people.

As Gus parked the bus a few hundred yards away from the imposing ark, Fr. Steven cautioned the people about the interior displays and placards that they would be seeing, reminding them that the fundamentalist

131

Christians who undertook this admirable project also promote their way of interpreting such things as the exact dates of the flood and the creation of the world, and their dismissal of the theory of evolution. "Our Catholic understanding of the great flood and Noah's Ark allows for a broader interpretation of these pre-historical events found in the Sacred Scriptures," he explained. "We try to reconcile the actual event with the mythical dimensions that may have shaped the telling of the story in the oral tradition."

Susan looked over her seat to see if her children understood anything of what Fr. Steven was saying, but they were looking out of the window, transfixed by the enormous replica of the ark.

"After you've had about an hour, or so, to tour the ark, we'll meet at Emzara's Kitchen for lunch at twelve-thirty," Susan directed the pilgrims. "It's the cafeteria building at the far end."

As the pilgrims got off the bus, Susan and Edward handed them their tickets. They broke up into smaller groups, couples and families as they walked the lengthy path toward the ark with the hundreds of other people visiting that day. Fr. Steven waited for Edward and Susan to finish distributing the tickets, so that they could walk the three levels of the interior of the ark together and he could answer any questions the children might have.

The people entered near the middle of the gigantic boat, up a ramp and through the broad doorway, similar to a barn door. Susan and Edward, with their children, and Fr. Steven were the last of their group to enter the cavernous interior of the ark. "Where did you hear all that about the lumber company in West Mifflin?" Edward asked his wife as they ambled along.

"My Dad told me," Susan said. "He worked most of his life in the lumber yard outside of Boonesboro. He took a keen interest in the building of this replica from the beginning. He knew about wood," she said. "He had great respect for the craftsman- ship of those Amish carpenters."

Barbara pulled on her mother's hand to walk around and see the animal cages. Edward and Fr. Steven walked with Bobby along the wall of the ark, lined with bags of feed, jugs and tools, stopping to read the placards explaining how Noah and his family managed the husbandry of so many different pairs of animals. Susan saw her pilgrims disperse in various directions; she knew there was no way she could keep them all in sight. Some were already mingled in the crowd, others had started up the ramp, and still others were waiting by the elevators to tour from the top level down. Susan explained to Barbara how each stall was equipped with a water trough and feed tray to sustain the animals.

"The straw on the floor is like at the zoo," Barbara said, having been to the Pittsburgh Zoo with her family a few weeks earlier.

Edward glanced across the bow of the ark to try and keep his wife and daughter in view, but with so many people milling about it was difficult and he lost them for several minutes.

The displays were similar on both sides except for the family living quarters where Susan and Barbara stopped to see a kind of hearth and suspended cooking pot, some raised platforms that looked like beds, and a few stools around a wooden table set with plates. Edward recognized Susan and Barbara standing there from behind. He couldn't call to them across the wave of tourists, so he led Bobby and Fr. Steven through the moving crowd. When they caught up with them they were beginning to move on to the next row of displays.

"Do you want to go to the second level now?" Edward asked Susan.

"There's something special there I want to show Barbara," Susan said loud enough for her daughter to overhear.

"What is it?" the little girl asked excitedly.

"You'll see," her mother teased her.

"Let's take the ramp," Bobby said and started toward the wide inclined walkway in the middle of the ark.

"Father?" Ed asked.

"Sure," the young priest answered. "I'm game."

So the five of them ascended the ramp slowly while Bobby tried to quicken their pace. "C'mon, you slow-pokes,"

"Take your time, Bobby." Susan said to her son.

"Noah had to wait for the flood waters to recede for several months before they could venture out onto the dry land." Fr. Steven added.

Bobby looked quizzically at their priest, then slowed his pace in response to his mother's instruction.

When they got to the second level Susan led little Barbara to where a large group of people were gathered near what looked like a miniature corral.

"Do you want to take a pony ride, Barbie?" Susan asked her daughter.

"Really?" the little girl said.

"There's a line; we'll have to wait."

"That's okay," Barbara said. "I can wait."

When the others caught up to them, they read the sign advertising children's rides on Shetland ponies for five dollars. Bobby looked up at his father. "You're too big," Edward said. "You have to be seven or younger—your feet would drag on the ground."

"The line's pretty long," Susan said. "Why don't you go ahead and we'll catch up with you on the third level."

"Okay," Edward said to his wife. "Have fun, Barbie," he said as he stroked his daughter's head.

When they got closer to the corral, Barbara could see the two shaggy Shetland ponies, one tan and the other brown, walking about with children in the saddles. An adult holding the reins led the darling horses around the corral.

"That one looks like Princess," Barbara said to her mother, pointing to the tan one that resembled her unicorn, her favorite stuffed animal.

"You're right, honey," Susan encouraged her little girl. "We'll make sure you get a ride on her."

The wait was about fifteen minutes before Susan handed the money to the attendant and another lifted Barbara into the saddle atop the beautiful pony with the shaggy blond hair. As he led the small horse around the corral, Susan could see the joy in her daughter's face. She took out her digital phone to get a picture of Barbara as she rode by holding onto the saddle horn for balance. The little girl waved to her mother with delight, holding on with her other hand. The brief ride was over in a few minutes but Barbara was thrilled.

"Did you get a picture, Mom?" she asked. "I want to show Daddy."

"Sure did, honey," Susan said and showed her the picture on her phone.

"C'mon," she said and pulled her mother toward the ramp. "Let's catch up with them."

Meanwhile, Edward, Bobby and Fr. Steven were making their way around the third level of the ark, which included some smaller bird cages and a window that opened to the sky at the very top of the ship. Some of the other parish pilgrims had joined them when they saw Fr. Steven.

After passing by more empty bird cages, Bobby stopped dead in his tracks when he came to a large cage with a model of a big bird that looked like a prehistoric pterodactyl, a dinosaur.

"It's a Thunderbird," he said, looking over his shoulder toward his father.

"A Thunderbird, Dad, like Grandpap said. I didn't know they were in the Bible, Father."

Edward and Fr. Steven didn't know what to say to Bobby. How could they explain why a dinosaur, that Bobby mistook for the legendary Thunderbird of American lore, was included in this fundamentalist display of Noah's ark? They were speechless before the anachronism.

"Grandpap said he saw one flying over an open field once when him and his friends were walking along the railroad tracks," Bobby repeated his grandfather's story.

"You sure it wasn't a big turkey vulture?" Edward said, trying to defuse the story.

"No," Bobby said. "Grandpap said they hid under a tree when it swooped down like it was going to snatch up one of them. He said its body was as big as me, the wings twice as long as an eagle's. That's the Thunderbird," the boy insisted, pointing again toward the teradactyl in the cage.

"I'll let you explain that one, Father," Edward said.

"Too many layers of biblical theology, primordial history and American folklore for me to untangle."

Just then, Susan and Barbara came up behind them.

"Daddy, Daddy, I rode a pretty pony," Barbara said and jumped into her father's arms. "Show him, Mommy, show him."

Susan showed him the picture on her cell phone of Barbara riding the Shetland pony in the corral.

Edward congratulated his daughter, happy to have a distraction from his son's complicated assertion. "You're a regular Kentucky horsewoman," he said and kissed her cheek.

"We better be going to lunch, now," Susan said. "They'll be waiting; it's almost twelve-thirty."

"But what about the Thunderbird?" Bobby pleaded.

"We'll discuss it at lunch," Fr. Steven said and put his arm around the boy's shoulder as they turned around to leave along with the pilgrims who had followed them to the third level.

By the time the little troop had descended the ramps and approached the large cafeteria, the rest of the pilgrims were standing in front of Emzara's Kitchen listening to the bluegrass band playing on the patio. Bobby and Barbara ran toward the music. The musicians were playing bluegrass melodies unfamiliar to most of the

Pittsburgh pilgrims but common enough to the locals. One played a banjo, another a steel guitar with rings on his fingers, a third played a washboard and the last a harmonica. "That sounds like the music Grandpap played," Barbara said to Bobby as she intently gazed at the harmonica player.

After a couple more melodies, the band took a break. The dozens of people listening broke into spontaneous applause. Some placed bills in the bucket marked "Donations."

The pilgrims entered the building and fell into the long line of hungry people waiting to have lunch. The cafeteria could seat a few hundred people and most of the tables were full. When they finally got to the buffet, they weren't disappointed. The children wanted the pizza and macaroni 'n' cheese, while the adults chose between meatloaf with mashed potatoes, pork chops with gravy, or vegetable lasagna. The cold beverages were in bottles or cans. Susan helped slide Barbara's tray along the counter to the cash register.

"These five are together," Edward said to the cashier and indicated his family and Fr. Steven.

"Thanks," Fr. Steven said. "You don't have to do that."

"We want to," Susan said as she grabbed more napkins.

After Edward paid the cashier, they walked around the perimeter of the large dining hall until they found an empty table that could accommodate the five of them comfortably. They saw several of the pilgrims scattered throughout the room.

"So, Father," Bobby started. "What do you think about the Thunderbird in the ark?"

"Let Father enjoy his lunch," Edward said to his son. "You can discuss it on the bus ride to Covington."

"Okay," Bobby said, a little disappointed but happy with his pizza.

When they went outside after lunch, Edward asked Susan and the children to wait on the park bench while he looked over the ark, the largest timber structure in the world. Fr. Steven went ahead to join the other pilgrims at the bus.

"Let him go," Susan said to her children, holding the tired Barbara and placing her free hand atop Bobby's on the bench. "He needs to do this."

Edward walked the length of the five-hundred foot ark, from stem to stern, marveling at the massive sea-worthy design in its breadth and height, formidable enough to survive a tumultuous deluge. He had been fascinated with the ark from the first moment he saw it, anticipating the opportunity to inspect the hull.

After a while, when Susan saw that most of the other pilgrims were headed back to the bus, she told Bobby to get his father, who had stopped by the ramp leading to the large entrance.

Edward was mumbling to himself and shaking his head slightly as they walked back to the bus; Susan noticed his preoccupation.

"C'mon," one of the pilgrims called to the Baudry family. "We're taking a picture with the ark in the background."

Once all forty of the pilgrims were positioned for the picture, they asked Gus to take it. He moved a few of them to the front, so they could all fit into the shot. After the main picture, others took photographs on their cell phone cameras.

As the bus pulled out of the parking lot, Edward leaned across the aisle. "Father, were the Hebrews good shipbuilders?"

"No, in fact, they lacked ship building skills and nautical talent," Fr. Steven explained. "Unlike the Greeks, the Romans and the Egyptians, the Hebrew people didn't venture out onto the Mediterranean—they were mostly leery of the sea except for the lakes and rivers around the Promised Land."

"Then, how could they have designed such a solid, seaworthy vessel as the ark?" Edward asked rhetorically. "I thought it was more myth than history."

"Well, Noah and his sons may have built it," Fr. Steven said. "But God was the architect, I guess." "I guess," Edward repeated.

While Edward and Father Steven were discussing the building of the ark, Susan thought again about their not having taken her children to her father's funeral last year. While they were close to the cemetery where her parents were buried outside of the Daniel Boone National Forest, they weren't close enough to divert their tour bus and visit their gravesites. The pilgrims would lose a couple of hours on their way to Covington, so she couldn't ask Father Steven for a favor. But she resolved to bring her family back to Kentucky next year to pray at her parents' graves and beautify the plots of earth that bore the Sutton name. She knew it would help her children have closure, too.

On the ride to Covington, the pilgrims were more subdued than usual following the long walk to and from the ark, let alone the tour through the three levels of the massive vessel. Besides, Noah's wife had served them an ample lunch in her 'kitchen' which further quieted most of them as the bus rumbled along the highway. And some of the pilgrims were already becoming nostalgic as they realized they were heading for the final stop on their tour of Catholic Kentucky.

Fr. Steven was thinking about his homily for their Mass at the beautiful Basilica of the Assumption of the Blessed Virgin Mary in Covington. He hoped to highlight key features of the pilgrimage and explain the unique significance of the impressive Church. He was aware that, at times, he could be a little pedantic, but he couldn't pass up an opportunity to teach the theology and history of the faith. He took the microphone out of its holder on the dashboard.

"Before we get to the Basilica in Covington," he began, "I want to alert you to be sure to appreciate the artistry and architecture in this magnificent church. The carving on the pews, the gorgeous terrazzo floors, the stone columns, the marble altar, the mosaics and paintings and, finally the stained-glass window, from floor to ceiling, in honor of the Blessed Mother's Assumption," he continued. "The largest stained glass church window in the world, in Kentucky, of all places." He was pleased with his recollection of the artistic features from the brochure.

Susan had never been in the Basilica and was looking forward to Mass. She felt a swell of pride that her home state housed such a beautiful church and the premier stained-glass window in honor of the Mother of God. The pilgrimage had awakened her deep love for Kentucky and, with that, the cherished memory of her father, Hiram. She recalled how he lamented the irony of his ending his days in smokey Pittsburgh, the gateway to the west, 'where anybody with any horse sense would've just kept on going to Kentucky.' Though Pittsburgh had long ago stopped being the steel making center of the country, she couldn't help but smile at her father's wit and wisdom, his love for their 'old Kentucky home,' as the song goes, and how he had bred that love into his children.

When Gus finally pulled the motor coach into the Basilica parking lot an hour, or so, after they had left the ark, most everybody was ready to stretch their legs. Again, Fr. Steven and Bobby went ahead to prepare for Mass. Edward helped the weary travelers out of the bus as Susan directed them up the few steps and into the Church. A docent met them at the door and led them to the front pews.

Sitting quietly, the pilgrims could not help but notice the imposing stained glass window off to their left that Fr. Steven had talked about on the bus. With the daylight illuminating the colorful panels of the window, Jesus crowned His assumed mother Queen of Heaven as a host of angels and saints looked on in wonder. They barely had time to notice some of the other features that Fr. Steven mentioned, before the soft bell signaled the beginning of Mass.

Fr. Steven's liturgical demeanor was especially solemn, enunciating the prayers and readings with clarity and purpose. In this magnificent Basilica and at the conclusion of his first parish pilgrimage, Fr. Steven wanted Mass to be a deep and spiritual experience for the forty people who had followed him into the former Kentucky frontier. For him, the trip had been an excursion into an American wilderness.

When he finished the gospel, the people sat down and he began his homily.

"I want to thank all of you for coming with us on this initial parish pilgrimage—I hope to take more trips in the future as a way to enhance the spiritual life of St. Mary's. You have been attentive and respectful and I could tell how much you enjoyed yourselves," Fr. Steven paused. "I especially want to thank Susan and Edward Baudry for all their help in planning and executing our pilgrimage. I couldn't have done it without them." The people had the good sense not to clap in church.

"In 431 A.D.," he started again, "the Council of Ephesus declared that the Blessed Virgin Mary was the 'Theotokos,' the God-bearer in Greek, or Mother of God. That church council followed a hundred years of debate in the patristic era about Jesus Christ as true God and true man, as we pray in the Nicean Creed. That beautiful stained glass window to your left," he pointed for effect, "was built in this Basilica of the Assumption to memorialize that teaching of the Church so that future generations of the faithful would recall Mary's unique role in salvation history. Besides the saints and angels gathered around Jesus and Mary in heaven, beneath them in those panels nearly reaching the floor, are the images of the theologians and doctors of the Church who contributed to the development of our Marian doctrine." Fr. Steven was excited in his spontaneous delivery. "They represent the living tradition of the Church, inspired by the Holy Spirit, who

145

develops the Church's teaching from the trajectory revealed in the Bible." Fr. Steven couldn't tell if he had lost some of the pilgrims. "That window is a kind of visual theology that teaches and preserves the profound truths of our Catholic faith."

After a few comments about the other beautiful appointments and master craftsmanship in the church, Fr. Steven moved on to catalogue the highlights of the pilgrimage: from Churchill Downs to the Basilica of St. Joseph, from the Abbey of Gethsemeni to the Maker's Mark Distillery, from the Ark to this Basilica, and the hospitality they met along the way from so many wonderful people.

The young priest concluded his sermon with "how fitting it is that our pilgrimage from St. Mary Parish should end in this Basilica dedicated to the Assumption of the Blessed Virgin Mary into Heaven."

Though he was quite animated during the homily, Fr. Steven recaptured the solemnity of the Mass as he had begun, determined to offer perfect praise to God. He prayed the Liturgy of the Eucharist fervently, especially the words of consecration. The sign of peace became an extended expression of the bond the pilgrims had formed the past three days. When they came forward for communion, Fr. Steven thought he detected tears in some of the people's eyes.

After Mass, the docent welcomed the group and began pointing out some of the beautiful features of the

Basilica that Fr. Steven had mentioned in his homily, and others that he had missed. She fielded a question about the difference between a Basilica and a Cathedral, or, in this case, how this church was designated both. She walked the group around the church to let them see, up close, the masterfully carved Stations of 58 the Cross.

"You stole her thunder," Edward said to Fr. Steven when he rejoined the group as the docent was briefly discussing the famous stained glass window. Bobby's ears perked up when he overheard his father say 'thunder.' But, he would have to wait for the long ride across Ohio for that explanation.

When they got back on the bus, Barbara asked her mother why they called Mary 'the tokless' and what did it mean. Susan explained the best she could and taught her daughter the correct Greek pronunciation: "Theo-to-kos."

After a while, the bus full of pilgrims crossed the Ohio River into Cincinnati as they began the long last leg of their ride home on Interstate 70 to Pennsylvania. Her duties as bus captain completed, Susan snuggled up to Edward and he put his arm around her with tenderness. "I love everything about you," he whispered to his wife. From somewhere in the middle of the coach, where the choir was sitting, the first soft lyrics rose in the jostling bus: "Well, I come from Alabama with my banjo on my knee/ and I'm bound for Louisiana, my own true love for to see/ Oh, Susannah, oh don't you cry for me/ 'cause I come from Alabama with my banjo on my knee." The voices rose as they sang the remembered rounds together, gaining voices and volume with each verse directed toward the front of the bus.

"They're singing to you, babe," Edward whispered.

In the arms of her beloved, with the sweet voices of her children singing behind her, Susan smiled and closed her eyes, confident that everything would be alright with her family, with her, with her 'Daddy,' as they left behind that enchanted land brought to life for her kids through the stories of her deceased father, the same songs and stories he had lovingly whispered in her ear, too.

Jimmy Patterson

The two friends walked the few damp blocks to the small Cathedral through the hundreds of young people amassing for the march along Market Street toward the Kiel Hockey Arena. Once inside the warm crowded church, they found a pew with a couple of empty seats down the center aisle. After settling in for quiet prayer, amidst the dozens of votive candles burning before various statues of saints, Michael got up.

"Excuse me, John," he said. "I have to go to the bathroom."

Michael walked back up the center aisle, assuming that he would find the rest rooms in the vestibule. When he got there, he surveyed the space looking for the lavatories. Then he noticed the young man in the jean jacket, who spoke with them at the base of the Arch, fumbling with some pamphlets at the book-wrack. Michael went into the men's room.

Returning to their pew, he mentioned to John that he had seen the young man, again, in the vestibule. While they took note of the sighting, neither of them thought much of the coincidence.

After several more minutes, they got up and left the church, careful to pick up a couple of the tri-fold brochures prominently displayed in the vestibule that highlighted the Pope's three-day visit to St. Louis. Upon leaving the older cathedral, they were immediately swallowed up amidst the hundreds of young people streaming up the wise avenue toward the arena. John and Michael were glad to be walking with the close crowd on this chilly, winter day.

"It says the Pope is supposed to get to the arena at 1 pm for the Youth Rally," Michael read from the brochure as they ambled up the street.

"Do we need tickets to get in?" John asked.

"Yeah," Michael said. "But all I got were the two tickets for the Papal Mass tomorrow at the Trans World Dome."

"That's too bad," John said. "He connects with young people; it would've been good to see the interaction."

They continued walking with the thousands of youth and young adults who were gathering for the rally. The marchers were nearly twenty across and already several blocks long. Michael and John stayed in the middle of the crowded street until they noticed some commotion on the sidewalk in the block ahead.

"What's that?" John said.

"C'mon," Michael said and started to angle through the marchers toward what appeared to be some kind of conflict the closer they got. They could hear two men arguing loudly above the rustle of the marchers.

"Throw that garbage away!" the one said, waving what appeared to be a handful of paper pamphlets.

"Rome's the whore of Babylon," the other countered, his face red and contorted in anger.

"Don't hand this trash to my kids," the other said and threw the pamphlets to the street.

As they neared the onlookers witnessing the confrontation, John picked up one of the pamphlets that had been tossed aside. The cover depicted a simple line drawing of Pope John Paul II with the dates of the papal visit to St.Louis, but when he opened it John saw a distorted image of the Pope with horns coming out of his mitre and a demon's tail extending from under his vestments.

Some marchers stepped between the two men before their argument could escalate into a physical confrontation.

Michael and John found themselves right behind the man who had thrown the pamphlets in the street as he tried to regain his composure. He was about their age. "Are you alright?" Michael asked him.

"That son of a _____tried to give those pamphlets to the kids in our youth group," he lamented. "At first, I thought they were itineraries, but when I opened it up they were really anti-Catholic propaganda."

"Yeah," John said. "I saw the inside, too."

"I'm responsible for these kids," the man said, still visibly upset at the confrontation. "I wish I had kept my cool in front of the students, though."

"Well," Michael tried to reassure him. "At least they saw you defending the faith." "They're here to rally with the Pope," the youth leader explained. "Not fend off attacks on their faith."

"How many did you bring?" John asked.

"Twenty-five," the man said. "But a few of them couldn't make it. Are you going to the Kiel, too?"

"We would," Michael said. "But we don't have tickets."

"Hey, I have a coujple extra," the man said and reached into his jacket pocket.

"You can have them," he said and handed the tickets to Michael.

"Thanks for helping calm me down."

"Thank you for the tickets," Michael and John said.

"See you inside," the man said and hurried to catch up with his teenagers.

As they watched him merge into the moving crowd, Michael and John both noticed the young man in the jean jacket and the red ball cap from earlier that day standing on the pavement on the other side of the street.

"That's him," Michael said.

"Yeah," John said as the young man turned away into the crowd. "That's him, alright."

"Do you think he's been following us?" Michael asked.

"It sure seems so," John said as they moved with the crowd, again. "Do you think he's FBI, or something?"

"The priest said we might be on some kind of watch list because of the late arrangements." Michael said facetiously. "We should give him a name." How about 'Jimmy'?" John said.

"Yeah," Michael said. "Jimmy Patterson—agent extraordinaire."

So the two friends walked a few more blocks with the swelling crowd of marchers, looking for the suspicious young man they had given the pseudonym.

"There's a warming station just ahead a few blocks," John said, noting the place on the brochure map. "I could go for a cup of coffee."

"Yeah," Michael agreed. "We still have a couple of hours before the Pope arrives." So, they veered off onto Tenth Street and walked a short distance to the parklet set aside for the marchers on this damp, winter morning.

A small group of about two hundred, or so, were in the parklet, some sipping coffee, others hot chocolate. There were two large heaters radiating warmth into the open space; some of the children and teens huddled

near the heaters. Michael and John found the hospitality table in the middle of the parklet.

"What's that sweet taste in the coffee?" John said after a couple of sips.

"I think they might add chicory to the coffee down
here," Michael said having been to St.Louis on a couple
of business trips. "It's alright," he said and took another
hot sip.

"So, how long do you think he has left?" John aske as
they moved toward an opening in the crowd.

"He's been the Pope for about twenty-five years already," Michael said.

"If he hadn't been shot who knows—he might have
lived to a hundred. He's a tough old Polak."

"There's not another Christian leader in the world
with his charisma," John said, sipping his coffee. "When
I hear him speak, I can hear the apostolic authority in
his voice."

"It'll be great to see him with the young people in the
arena," Michael said and took another swallow of coffee. "When he was in the Phillipines for World Youth
Day some years ago, over six million people gathered in
the national park to be a part of the papal Mass. I think
it was the largest gathering of people for any event in
the twentieth century, let alone for Mass."

"I'm glad we made it here," John said and then
glanced toward one of the raised platforms at the corner
of the parklet. "Mike, look up there."

"You're right," Michael said, noting the red ball cap and jean jacket.

"That's our Jimmy."

"He's looking right at us," John said. "Now, he's pointing us out to that guard standing next to him."

"Do you believe that?" Michael said incredulously. "I guess we look like some kind of terrorists drinking coffee in the park."

"He gives me the creeps," John said and started walking away from the open space to mingle with the crowd.

"He's just doing his job," Michael said. "We're probably his assignment. But between the two of us, I doubt we even have an outstanding parking ticket."

"I might have one," John said.

"This is crazy," Michael said, looking back over his shoulder to catch a glimpse of Jimmy still eyeing them from the platform.

"Do you think he'll follow us into the arena?" John wondered aloud.

"He's been following us all morning," Michael observed. "Why would he stop now?"

After they finished their coffee, Michael and John decided to reenter the march and wait for the Pope inside the Kiel Arena now that they had tickets. Along the way, they kept looking over their shoulders for 'Jimmy,' but the could not spot him. Inside, they found their seats near the youth leader and the teenagers, about hald-way up the stands. It felt good to be in the warm area. Then the sound system announced that there was a delay and the Pope would not arrive until after 2 pm. So, Michael and John started into the conversation about his upcoming marriage.

"I don't know," Michael said. "Ever since my sister's divorce, marriage seems so risky. I thought her and Peter were made for each other. I like the guy, too. We went fishing a few times."

"You can't be afraid of marriage because your sister got divorced," John said.

"Yeah, but it really broke her up," Michael said. "She was an emotional wreck for a year after he left her. Thank God there were no kids."

"Maybe that was the problem," John said. "No children to keep them together."

"I don't know," Michael said. "I just can't see myself settling down, at least not yet."

"You just haven't found the right woman," John said.

So they talked for an hour, or so, about John's upcoming wedding to Lisa, about their friends from school who had gotten married, some living together, others already divorced while they waited for Pope John Paul II, amidst the fifteen thousand young people intermittently chanting "John Paul II, we love you," whenever the image of his approaching motorcade flashed on the big screen above the stage.

From time to time, one or the other of them would scan the crowd to look for 'Jimmy,' but to no avail. Finally, when the Pope came into the arena waving from the open roof of the popemobile, the crowd stood up and became raucus, cheering and clapping for the man they saw as a spiritual rockstar. It was like and electric current had coursed through the crowd, including Michael and John.

The enthusiastic crowd continued to chant while the Pope in his white cassock was helped up the stairs to the stage and microphone. After several minutes, the youth finally quieted down to enable the Pope to say something. Ever the actor, John Paul's first words were a rhythmic response to the thunderous chanting of the crowd: "John Paul II, he loves you!" which set them into another round of cheers and chants.

Michael and John smiled at each other, realizing that witnessing this dynamic was why they had come to St.Louis. The hour-long prayer, singing and preaching, began with a presentation of a St. Louis Blues hockey stick and Jersey to the Pope from a few of the representatives from the various youth groups. "JPII" was emblazoned on the back of the jersey with the number "1." The Pope further demonstrated his keen stage awareness, when he handed his crozier to one of his attendants and took a simulated slap shot with the hockey stick they had given him. All the youth roared in delight with his timely gesture. Eventually, the Pope began his prepared remarks, captivating the thousands of young people with his every word in his thick, Polish accent. He called them to be witnesses of hope in the new millennium, bringing the gospel of life and love toe every aspect of their lives: family, friends, school, leisure and work. He spoke with a credible sympathy that seemed to strike a chord in each young person, as if he, somehow, knew them. Michael and John had all but forgotten about 'Jimmy,' as they were enthralled by the Pope's oration like everyone else in the arena. When John Paul completed his inspirational talk, he was met with another thunderous round of cheers, chants and applause that escorted the popemobile on its way out of the arena.

Walking back to their hotel, Michael and John talked about the dynamic rapore the Pope had with the young people and the encouraging words he spoke to them, like he was sending them off to battle. They were both hungry and, after a stop in their room, went downstairs to the lobby restaurant for an early supper. They had a few Budweisers with their meal.

When they got back to their room, Michael started fumbling around the top of the dresser where the men had laid out their incidentals like keys and wallets.

"John, did you see my notebook?" Michael asked his friend.

"No," John said.

"I swore I left it here on the dresser," Michael said. Eventually he opened the drawer on the nightstand between their beds and found his journal next to the Gidean Bible.

"I know I didn't put it in here."

"I didn't touch it," John said.

"Then, who did?" Michael asked rhetorically.

"You don't think, they had access to our room, do you?" John said.

"Why not," Michael said. "We were out all day. I don't think it was housekeeping."

"If somebody was in here," John said. "The journal would have been the first thing they searched for whatever they were looking for."

"I just had notes about the trip," Michael said. "I started it back in Pittsburgh when we got the tickets from Fr. Alfred."

"Do you think that priest is under suspicion, too?" John said.

The two men laughed aloud when they thought of the innocent, old priest drawing the investigative interest of the FBI, or some local agency.

"But wouldn't they have put it back where they found it?" John suggested.

"Unless Jimmy's colleagues wanted ut to know they were here and had their eye on us," Michael said. "Do you think they tapped the phone?" John said. "The only call I made was to Lisa when we arrived."

"I wouldn't be surprised," Michael said.

As John cleaned up and changed for bed, Michael sat at the small desk and made an entry into his journal about the day's events. He included mention of 'Jimmy Patterson,' as well as the Pope, the interview, the march, the conflict on the street, and especially the amazing interaction at the Youth Rally in the Kiel Arena. When he completed the entry, he was careful to place it atop the dresser where he had put it originally.

He changed, shut off the desk lamp, and was asleep in a few minutes after his head hit the pillow.

The next morning, they rose leisurely; the papal Mass was not until 12 noon at the Trans World Dome just a block, or so, from their hotel. They watched some of the local television coverage of the papal visit, including the Youth Rally at the Kiel Arena.

When Michael took his shower, John called Lisa at the station to ask what she thought of the interview, which she liked, adding that he looked distinguished with this beard.

Once Michael finished in the bathroom, John went in to shave, brush his teeth and shower.

Michael sat at the desk expanding on his journal entry from last night, commenting more about 'Jimmy' than on the Pope. When they were dressed, they gathered their wallets, keys and coats and took the elevator downstairs to the lobby restaurant for brunch. They both ordered the BLT special with a side of french fries.

They washed down their sandwiches with coffee and a glass of water.

"You have the tickets?" John asked Michael as they stepped out onto the pavement to walk the short distance to the Trans World Dome.

"They're right here in my pocket," Michael said and tapped his coat atop his heart. Hundreds of other pilgrims were also swarming toward the Dome.

The uniformed security guards at the entrances were checking the backpacks, shoulder bags and purses of everyone who entered. The line at the gates moved slowly. Michael and John were asked to open their coats before they handed their tickets to the usher who tore off the stub and gave them the colorful part of the ticket with the imprint of the papal keys. "You're in Section 352, row RR, way up top," the man said.

So, the two of them walked up the several ramps along with the thousands of others to the top level of the domed stadium, picking up programs along the way. When they finally found their seats, they could see that the place was already nearly full.

"How many people does this hold?" John asked.

"One hundred and ten thousand," Michael said.

"And they're all here," John said, delighted that they were among the throng of pilgrims who had journeyed to St. Louis, from near and far, to be a part of this historic celebration.

Michael stood up at their seats to survey the people in their section.

"You looking for Jimmy?" John asked his friend.

"They got our seat numbers" Michael said. "They probably know what we had for brunch."

After awhile, some organ prelude music could be heard on the speakers throughout the stadium. The music quieted the crowd anticipating the opening of the Papal Mass. While Michael knew the first verse of the opening hymn, John had to follow along with the program, though he recognized the familiar melody. The Pope, in a booming baritone voice, began the Mass from his presider's chair with the sign of the cross, including the Holy Trinity. The order of the Catholic Mass was not so different from the Anglican worship that John was used to. After the reading from Saint Paul's letter to the Romans, a vested deacon read the Gospel about the wedding at Cana and Jesus' first miracle changing water into wine. Then Pope John Paul II walked to the lectern with the help of his metal staff topped with a crucifix.

Following some introductory remarks, the Pope launched into a powerful homily about marriage, the place of the family in God's plan for salvation, the complementarity of the genders, and the precious gift of human life that God entrusts to mothers and fathers. John was thrilled to hear this Christian leader he admired so much speaking eloquently about marriage with his own wedding just several months away in June. Unlike at the Kiel Arena, the people remained quiet throughout his homily, maintaining the decorum of the liturgy. The Pope spoke with passion in his halting English about the noble vocation of marriage and the bond of love that holds husbands, wives and children together as God intends. Michael noticed a young couple nearby holding hands throughout the Pope's talk, the woman with tears on her face. He spoke for nearly a half hour in his thick accent, at times diverging from his prepared remarks. When he finished, a spontaneous round of applause rose from the 110,000 people seated in the Dome.

Yellow and white banners and flags, the papal colors, adorned the makeshift sanctuary, the altar highlighted with flower arrangements that Michael and John could barely see from their height in the top section of the indoor stadium. Despite their distance, Michael and John were riveted to the Pope's words and actions a he proceeded to pray the Eucharistic Prayer of the Mass. At the consecration, the Pope made an effort to show the consecrated host and the chalice of the precious blood to everyone with a sweeping arc from one side of the altar to the other. The Lord's Prayer brought the people to their fee as they prayed together the most familiar prayer in Christiandom.

Michael sang the familiar Latin chant of 'Agnus Dei' with the throng. When it came time for communion, a few hundred priests and deacons fanned out into the Dome's aisles on every level of seating accompanied by an attendant holding a yellow and white umbrella to designate the communion station. Michael made his way to receive communion, while John remained seated in deference to his friend's faith.

It took almost an hour to distribute the Blessed Sacrament. Through it all, the Pope sat in a stoic meditation, absorbed in prayer as was his habit. With the Pope's final blessing, John found himself making the sign of the cross on his body along with Michael and the other 100,000 Catholic gathered in worship. Filled with joy, Michael and John moved slowly with the relatively quiet crowd down the ramps and out of the Trans World Dome. Once on the street, they began to talk excitedly about what they had just experienced.

"Hearing all of you chanting those ancient Latin verses was powerful," John said. "I haven't heard anything like that in years."

"He commanded that whole crowd." Michael said. "You could hear a pin drop during his homily."

"I needed to hear all that about marriage and family," John said as they crossed the avenue. "They never preach like that in our Church."

"Let's go up to the room for a pit stop," Michael said. "I saw a little Italian restaurant down the block."

"It's our last night," John said. "We should go out to celebrate."

So, after they stopped in their room on the fourth floor to freshen up, they ventured out to enjoy a good meal on the last night of their pilgrimage. They both liked Italian food.

"Luigi's," Michael read aloud the name of the restaurant as they entered.

"This looks like the little family place Lisa and I like to go to in Bloomfield," John said. "They have a mandolin hanging on the wall, too, and a similar mural of some Mediterranean seaside town."

"I hope the food's as good," Michael said. "I'm starving."

The restaurant was starting to fill up with the people leaving the Papal Mass, but Michael and John got a table almost immediately.

"Bring us a bottle of your house Chianti," Michael told the waiter sporting a thin moustache and a thin black tie on his white shirt.

"Do you like greens and beans?" John asked Michael as he looked over the appetizers on the menu. When Michael nodded in approval John said to the waiter: "The beans and greens with some sausage."

The waiter poured the first glasses of wine and waters and shortly afterwards brought the appetizer with some fresh Italian bread and a plate of olive oil with herbs. "Lisa, loves this stuff," John said. "We always get it. The two friends helped themselves to the generous plate of sautéed greens, white beans and slices of Italian sausage and dipped the bread into the oil and herbs.

"This is delicious," John said.

"Let's have a toast to the Pope," Michael said and raised his glass.

"A true apostle," John said as they clinked their glasses.

When the middle-aged waiter returned to their table, the men ordered their meals.

"How's the lasagna?" Michael asked the waiter.

"The chef makes it fresh everyday," he answered. "Good choice."

"With the chicken paustina soup," Michael added.

"I'll have the Fettucini Alfredo with a tossed salad and your house dressing," John ordered his meal.

"Put this on one check," Michael said as the waiter turned away.

"You don't have to do that," John said.

"Hey, I don't think I would have made it if you weren't so insistent," Michael said.

"This trip's been better than I would have ever imagined.

"He's an historic figure," John said.

"Maybe the greatest pope in the twentieth century," Michael said. "Now, even the twenty-first."

When the waiter returned with their food, he took away the empty plate of greens and poured them another glass of Chianti.

The two pilgrims ate their delicious meals voraciously, relishing every bite. They were satisfied with the meal as they were with the completion of their three-day pilgrimage. Though the food was heavy, they finished their ample plates, washing down the pasta dishes with the rest of the wine.

"Have you saved room for desert?" the waiter said when he returned to their table. "The canolis are made in-house."

"No, I'm full," John said.

"Me, too," Michael said. "Just the check."

As they drank their last glass of wine, a certain feeling of satisfaction settled on the two men.

"What do you think Jimmy had for supper?" John teased.

"I hope he gets indigestion," Michael said and chuckled.

Even after their heavy meals, the men were feeling the wine. They ambled back to their hotel. In their room, they packed their luggage and discussed their plans for an early departure the next day before they went to bed. Michael made a last entry in his journal and then fell into as sound a sleep as he had had in months.

The next morning, Michael and John were a little sluggish from the bottle of wine. After they washed and changed, they took their luggage to the lobby to check out. They got a coffee in the bistro and picked up

Mike's SUV in the parking garage. They planned on getting some breakfast once they were on the road.

Crossing the Mississippi was a kind of sign marking the end of their pilgrimage.

"I'm glad we made it," Michael said as they drove the length of the expansion bridge.

"I can't wait to tell Lisa all about it, " John said.

"We won't be doing this, again, anytime soon," Michael said alluding to the final road trip of their decades-long friendship.

"We had some fun," John said. "You remember that time we went to Canada to go fishing?"

"Yeah, and you almost drowned in that stream," Michael recalled and laughed with the memory.

"There he is," John said as they passed another billboard with a likeness of the Pope's face announcing the papal trip.

"Today, he's having Mass for the bishops, priests and deacons at the new cathedral outside of town," Michael said.

"Couldn't you get tickets for that one?" John teased his fried.

They enjoyed the friendly banter as they sped down the interstate on their way back to Pennsylvania. Along their way home, they would talk about 'Jimmy Patterson' almost as much as Pope John Paul II, though he was the reason they had traveled to Missouri.

Left Coast

"Do you want another cup of coffee?" Virginia asked her husband.

"Thanks, Ginnie," Walter said. "That pie was delicious."

"Apple was always John's favorite," she said, referring to their son. She poured them both another cup of coffee.

"When is our flight on Friday?" he asked.

"We leave for Chicago at one p.m.," she said. "Our flight to San Diego departs at three."

"I hope we don't get held up in that airport," Walter said, sipping his black coffee. "That place can be a mess."

"We should be in San Diego around nine p.m., their time," Virginia said, adding some cream and sugar to her cup of hot coffee.

"Is he picking us up?" Walter asked her, as she had made the arrangements.

"He and his girlfriend will meet us at the airport," she said. "I'm anxious to meet her. She sounds nice on the phone."

"Who names their daughter, Sky?" he said, referring to John's girlfriend of the past couple of years.

"Oh, Walter," she said. "Please don't pick a fight before we even get there."

"Well, she went to Berkley," Walter said. "Her parents were probably some tree-huggin' hippies."

Virginia tried to suppress her laughter. "She could be our daughter-in-law someday. She's the first girl he's been serious about since he got out of college."

As they continued to chitchat about their upcoming trip to San Diego later that week, Virginia began to clear the kitchen table of the plates, glasses, and utensils they used for their pot roast supper. Walter helped her, placing the platter of leftover meat and potatoes on the counter near the refrigerator.

"That was delicious, Ginnie," he said. "We better eat all the meat we can before Friday. Who knows what we'll get out there."

"They're vegetarians, not vegans," Virginia said. "I'm sure it'll be fine."

"I still think we should've stayed in a hotel," he said.

"We haven't seen him for two years," she said, rinsing off the greasy plates in the sink. "He offered for us to stay with them. We can't be ungracious."

"But they're not married," Walter said and dutifully placed the rinsed plates, cups, glasses, and utensils in the dishwasher.

"I know," she said. "But maybe we can help them see the importance of marriage. I think he really likes this girl."

"He better," Walter said. "They've been living together for the past year."

"Don't you have to get ready for your meeting?" she said, clearing off the table.

"It's not 'til seven," he said. "It's the Cleveland area regional meeting of Serra. I don't have to chair this one."

"Well, you should still put on a sportcoat," Virginia said. "You're a tenured professor at a prestigious Catholic university. You may be asked to say something."

"You're right," he said. "But sometimes I wonder if John Carroll is even Catholic anymore. I still blame those Jesuits for John drifting away from the Church."

"A lot of young people question their faith these days," she said. "Maybe we can get them to come to Church with us while we're there. We'll be there on Sunday."

"You always defend him," Walter said, passing his hand over his shock of white hair. "Just because he's your youngest."

"He's our son, Walter," she said. "I'll always love him."

Over the next few days, as they prepared for their trip to California, Virginia took care of packing their clothing, toiletries, and medications, freeing Walter to finish the article he was writing for The American Historical Review, entitled 'Revisionism and the American Frontier.' Meanwhile, Virginia completed the embroidery on the pillow she had made for John and Sky, sewing their names in a graceful, blue script on the off-white pillow case. She was a skilled seamstress, too.

Their flights were uneventful except for having to wear the covid-19 face masks. They arrived in San Diego a little before nine p.m., West Coast time. Especially on the flight out of Chicago, Virginia noticed Walter becoming more pensive as he anticipated the weekend with John. Their last meeting in Cleveland had ended in a bitter argument. She readied herself to mediate the generational tension between father and son, between her staunch, Catholic husband and her progressive, agnostic son.

John and Sky were waiting for his parents in their hybrid Honda at the curbside pickup of the San Diego Airport. When he saw them coming out of the gate, he and Sky got out of the car to greet them. John wore a John Carroll golf shirt and blue jeans, while Sky had on a floral, printed dress. Virginia hurried to hug her son and then his pretty, young girlfriend whom she had only talked with on the phone. Walter, meanwhile, stood stoically behind her, extending his hand to John and, then, Sky, after Virginia's effusive greeting. John put their suitcases in the trunk as Sky showed his parents into the back seat.

"I'm so happy to finally meet you," Virginia said. "You're even prettier than John told us," noting Sky's blond hair that fell to her waist. "And your eyes match your name, dear."

"Thank you," Sky said, blushing. "It's good to meet you, too."

Walter and John were quiet on the ride to their duplex in San Marcos, while the women made small talk about the flight, the ideal weather, and the pandemic.

"Would you like to eat something?" Sky said once they were inside. "I made a banana nut bread that's still warm."

"It's delicious," John said. "She's a baker like you, Mom."

"I'm hungry," Walter complained. "All they gave us were peanuts on the plane and we had to wear those annoying masks."

So, the four of them sat at the dining room table that Sky had previously set. She poured the tea that had been steeping awhile while John got the butter, milk, and cream cheese from the refrigerator. The grapes and orange slices were already on the table.

"This is a green tea," Sky said. "There's some sugar or honey if you like."

John cut the warm loaf into thick slices and then served them to his parents and Sky.

"I like what you've done to the place," Virginia said. "The plants, the wall hangings, and the earth tones."

"That's her doing," John said. "She has a flair for that natural look."

"Isn't it so warm and cozy, Walter?" Virginia prompted her husband.

"Do you have to water the plants every day?" he asked Sky.

"Usually, every other day," Sky explained. "Except that cactus near the window. We show that one as little love as possible, and it still grows."

"This is delicious," Virginia said to Sky, enjoying her banana nut bread with a smear of cream cheese. "Did you use some honey in the recipe?"

"Yes," Sky said. "We get it from a local, organic farm, along with our eggs and dairy."

Walter and John ate their slices with the rich butter.

"Can I have another piece?" Walter asked Sky.

John quickly cut his father another slice and placed it on his plate.

So, the four of them talked politely over the evening snack, trying to become acquainted with each other, and in John's case, reacquainted. They finished the banana bread that Sky had made and most of the grapes and orange slices. After about an hour, or so, Virginia suggested that they were tired after flying across country and would like to go to bed. John carried their suitcases into the spare bedroom that Sky had prepared for them.

She mentioned that they had their own bathroom at the end of the hallway.

"Oh, wait, dear," Virginia said to Sky and opened her suitcase. "I made something for you." She handed her the pillow with their names embroidered on the cover.

"It's precious! Thank you, Mrs. Hinman," Sky said and held the pillow to her chest.

"Ginnie," she said. "Just call me Ginnie."

They hugged and Virginia kissed her on the cheek. Then she hugged and kissed her son, again.

"Thanks, Mom," John said.

Then they all said, "Goodnight."

Walter thanked the couple for their hospitality and was anxious to close the door to their room and go to sleep.

"This will look so nice on the bed," Sky said as they cleared off the dining room table. "Your mother is so sweet."

"Yes, she is," John said. "Professor Hinman can be a little formal."

"He seemed nice" Sky said. "I hoped they liked me."

"What's not to like," John said. You're beautiful, kind, intelligent, and you make a great banana nut bread." John hugged Sky and gave her a kiss.

"Well, I want to make a good first impression," Sky said. "They are your parents. And you said they weren't so happy about us living together."

"They're Catholic," John said. "They want us to get married."

"I want to get married, someday," Sky said. "I love you, John."

"And I love you, Sky," he said. "They'll be the first ones we tell when we get engaged."

They finished clearing the table and walked hand-in-hand to their bedroom.

As they changed clothing for bed, Sky said: "I feel a little self-conscious with your parents down the hall. Maybe we can just snuggle tonight, John." They kissed.

"Me, too," he said and put his arm around her, while she laid her head on his chest.

Mr. & Mrs. Hinman slept in later than usual due to the long flight to the West Coast. When they did get up after nine a.m., they showered and dressed for their first, full day in San Diego. Coming to the kitchen, Virginia looked especially fresh in the new blue dress she bought for the trip. Walter wore his usual dark trousers with a clean, white shirt.

"Good morning," John and Sky greeted his parents.

"Good morning, dears," Virginia said.

"G'mornin'" Walter mumbled.

John slid his mother's chair closer to the table.

"What smells so good?" Virginia asked. Did you bake bread?"

"A couple fresh loaves for later," Sky said. "For breakfast, we're having blueberry pancakes." Sky removed the lid that was keeping the first several warm. "You can get started while I cook the rest."

"There's butter, maple syrup, and honey," John said to his parents and filled their glasses with orange juice. "Freshly squeezed," he added.

"Pancakes were always our Saturday breakfast," Virginia said. "Blueberry are Walter's favorite."

"John told me," Sky said, as she flipped the hotcakes over on the griddle. "We picked the blueberries yesterday at the farm."

John served a couple of pancakes to each of his parents and to himself, putting the last two on Sky's plate with the lid to keep them warm.

"Here's some coffee," Sky said as she poured the steaming coffee into their cups. "It's Columbian."

"We ground the beans fresh this morning," John added.

Professor Hinman took a sip before he began to eat. "That's a good cup of coffee," he said, and took another sip.

Virginia added some cream and sugar to hers.

Sky took the empty platter to the stove for the rest of the pancakes. When she returned to the table she put the lid over the new batch.

"Well, dig in," Sky said. "You didn't have to wait for me."

"Can we say grace?" Walter said.

"Sure, Dad," John said, calling him the familiar term for the first time since his parents arrived.

Walter and Virginia made the sign of the cross before he led the traditional Catholic meal prayer. Virginia joined in prayer with him. John and Sky simply bowed their heads in silence and held hands.

They all ate the tasty pancakes with butter and maple syrup or honey. Sky pointed out the bowl of peach yogurt at the end of the table where his parents were sitting.

"This is delicious, dear," Virginia said, not bashful to ask for another and a couple more for Walter.

"I'm glad you're enjoying them," Sky said, happy that she was making John's parents feel welcomed in their home.

"Can I have another cup of that coffee?" Walter asked.

John got up to get the coffee pot and poured more into their cups.

Walter and Virginia were hungry after yesterday and ate heartily. Though not accustomed to eating yogurt, they both tried a dollop or two.

"That was delicious," Walter said.

"Yes it was," Virginia added. "I can see why John's so happy."

When they finished breakfast, they lingered at the table talking about the day's itinerary.

"I thought we might go to the Serra Museum, Dad," John said. "It's in the presideo at the Mission. It's an easy ride on a Saturday."

"That sounds good, John," Walter said, pleased that his son anticipated his interest in the initial California mission that St. Junipero Serra established at San Diego in 1769.

"While you two explore the museum," Virginia said, "I thought Sky and I could do a little shopping and have a nice luncheon. A lady's day." Virginia was hoping to bring father and son together, as well as to get to know Sky a little better. Her plan would kill two birds with one stone.

"I'd like that, too," Sky said, happy that John's kind mother wanted to be with her. "But I don't do a lot of shopping."

"My girlfriend told me to try the Westfield Mall for the boutiques and the Nordstrom's," Virginia said. "She recommended the Season's Restaurant, too. It'll be fun."

"I know where that's at," Sky said. "It's a little high end."

"Oh, don't fret" Virginia leaned closer to Sky and quietly reassured her with a chuckle. "The professor makes a handsome living at the University. My treat."

Walter perceived his wife's little scheme and thought it might help him and John make a 'rapprochement.'

"That sounds like we'll all have a good day. I'll certainly enjoy the museum."

"That's settled, then," John said, a little apprehensive about being alone with his father for the afternoon without his mother as a buffer. "We can leave about one o'clock and be back in time for supper. Sky has something special in store for you."

"I hope you like lentil soup," Sky said to John's parents. "That's why I made the homemade bread—to have with the soup."

"That sounds wonderful, dear," Virginia said, reassuringly, though she didn't make lentil soup herself.

Walter and John went into the living room to talk about one of their safe and common interests: baseball; while Virginia and Sky stayed in the kitchen clearing the table and getting to know each other better in that comfortable domestic setting.

"I never made lentil soup," Virginia said. "What are the ingredients?"

"Well, I already have the beans soaking," Sky said, as she put the milk and butter into the refrigerator. "The lentils are a good source of protein for us."

"Where do these go?" Virginia asked.

"You can put the syrup in the refrigerator," Sky said and held open the door. "The honey goes in the pantry cupboard."

"So, what else goes in the soup?" Virginia asked, again.

"Some vegetable stock," Sky explained. "Garlic, green peppers, carrots, onions, celery, salt and pepper, and a pinch of cayenne. It'll stew in the slow cooker while we're out for the day."

"I can help cut the vegetables," Virginia said.

"Oh, no," Sky said. "You're on vacation."

"Nonsense," Virginia teased. "I haven't cooked anything for John in a couple of years. I'd like to help."

So, Sky retrieved the peppers, carrots, onions, and celery from the vegetable crisper and got the wooden cutting board and a sharp knife for Virginia. "I'm not used to much help in the kitchen," she said.

"I know," Virginia said. "John takes after his father. But they're not shy about eating."

The women giggled in a kind of benign, feminine conspiracy against the men they loved.

As Virginia began slicing the vegetables, Sky got the garlic cloves, a frying pan, and placed the slow cooker on the counter. The older woman prompted the younger to explain how she made her lentil soup, step by step, though she had already surmised the process from her own experience of cooking soups and casseroles. The women were bonding, as Virginia had hoped.

Meanwhile, John and Walter were talking in the living room about baseball, one of the few topics they could discuss in recent years without ending in an argument.

"I was hoping that we could see a Padres game while were here," Walter said. "But they're not even playing any games until later in July because of the pandemic."

"I went to a few games last year," John said. "The Padres looked pretty good."

"The Indians picked up a couple of pitchers in the offseason that should strengthen their rotation," Walter said. "They have the hitting."

They talked some more about the relative strengths and weaknesses of the San Diego Padres and the Cleveland Indians until they exhausted the rosters. Then Walter brought up the issue that was riling the Cleveland fans that summer.

"Can you believe the management is talking about changing the name of the team?" Walter asked rhetorically. "They've been the Indians for a hundred years and now they want to change the name."

"I think it's in response to the nativist movement across the country," John said politely. "Out here, even Saint Junipero Serra has come under some scrutiny, too."

"That's just revisionist history," Walter said. "Serra served and organized the Indians in California, protecting them from the Spanish conquistadors."

Just when their discussion was about to turn into a debate, the women came into the room and sat down beside them. The father and son instinctively became quiet in deference to their women.

"While you two were talking about sports," Virginia said, "Sky taught me how to make lentil soup."

"You'll have to excuse me," Sky said. "I have to get cleaned up and changed; I've been cooking all morning."

"You go ahead, dear," Virginia said. "We have plenty of time."

So, with Sky taking a shower and getting ready for the outing with John's mother, the three of them were left in the living room to catch up and get reacquainted.

"I think Sky is precious, John," Virginia said. "She's so thoughtful and gracious, so considerate of us. And I can see being a vegetarian hasn't hurt you any; you've put on a few pounds. You look good, dear."

"She enjoys cooking," John said. "At first, I wasn't sure how I'd like being a vegetarian, but my health is good and she's a great cook. Wait 'til you taste her lentil soup."

"So, how's your work going with that consulting outfit?" Walter asked.

"Well, I just got a promotion," John said proudly." "I supervise the public opinion section. We do polls, surveys, and interviews to determine what people are thinking about the important issues of the day. Then we sell the results to political campaigns or groups for the use of their candidates."

"Is that lucrative?" Virginia asked.

"You'd be surprised, Mom," John said. "These days, the politicians are looking for any advantage. With the polarity among the electorate, they're looking at every nuance of the issues to appeal to their constituency."

"I take it that most of your clients are on the left," Walter said.

"Well, out here, Dad," John explained, "there are a lot of progressive thinking voters. But we have conservative clients, also. Our firm has a good reputation."

Virginia intuited where the conversation was going, so she deflected their dialogue to a more immediate subject.

"Are you thinking about asking Sky to get married?" she said to John, broaching the topic that was uppermost on their minds. "With your promotion, you should be in a better position to provide for a family."

"Well, we both like San Diego," John said. "And I did get a considerable raise."

"So, what are you waiting for, son?" Walter interjected.

John paused before he answered. "We're talking, now. When the time's right, I'll ask her; but don't say anything to her, yet."

Virginia got up from the couch to embrace her son in the cushioned chair where he was sitting. "She's the one," she said. "You'll never find a sweeter girl. I have a feeling about her."

"Your mother and her feelings," Walter said under his breath. "If you love her, don't dilly-dally, John. She's a beautiful young woman; she won't wait forever."

"I'm glad you two approve," John said, a little defensively, and repositioned himself in the upholstered chair when his mother returned to the couch. "I do love her; that's for sure."

So, now that they had broached that most important subject, the three of them fell into a more relaxed conversation about John's brother and sister and their families, about the ages of his nieces and nephews, about cousins who were getting married, about neighbors he remembered who had died in the past couple of years. There was so much to keep him abreast of, and Virginia was determined to keep him in the familial loop.

When Sky joined them in the living room, Virginia was quick to compliment her appearance. "You look so pretty, dear," she said. "I love that dress."

John noticed how charming she looked in her floral printed dress with the lace edging at the hem and short sleeves. "You look great, Sky," he said, though he was not one to give a lot compliments.

"We better hope some sailors don't try to whisk our girls off for a cruise across the sea," Walter said, in his attempt at some harmless humor.

They laughed at his uncharacteristic, friendly banter.

So, they talked a while more, his parents asking questions about their circle of friends, Sky's work at the non-profit environmental agency, their idyllic weather, and how often they get to the beach. The professor also mentioned the article he had just finished for publication in that academic journal. The conversation was purposefully innocuous, the Hinman's, with Virginia's lead, doing their best to maintain a friendly, familial ambience and avoiding any controversies during the few days they were staying with their son and his future fiancée.

When they were talked out, John suggested that it was time to get going for the afternoon's excursions. So, the ladies took off for the Westfield Mall in Sky's yellow Volks- wagon and the fellows for the Serra Museum in John's gray Honda.

On their drive to the museum, Walter was happy to expound on his article, while John was prudent enough to listen without posing any probing questions. The two of them talked politely along the highway, mindful of the last time they were together and got ensnared in a raucous argument. As they got close to the Serra Center, John was dreading the possibility of nativist protestors picketing in front of the museum as they had done intermittently over the past few years, before and since Saint Junipero Serra had been canonized by the Church. Fortunately, as they pulled into the parking lot, John saw no one except the typical tourists entering the presideo.

Meanwhile, Sky and Virginia were enjoying the ride to the mall, talking about what they might shop for, the boutiques, and the lunch they would indulge in, Virginia taking any opportunity to compliment the younger woman. She intuited that Sky seemed to delight in John's mother taking a genuine interest in what she had to say. The younger woman was hopeful that their cordial exchange would begin to build the kind of trust with John's family that would be essential if they were to get married someday. Virginia had that maternal way about her that encouraged Sky to relax and be herself, just as she had done with her own daughter when she was growing up.

At the small museum, John could see that his father was engrossed in the displays and placards about the life of Saint Junipero Serra and the first of his twenty-one missions that he established along the coast of Alta California, from San Diego to San Francisco. Even if he thought some of the information was more hagiography than history, John had the good sense not to spoil his father's idealized conception of the patron saint of the Catholic club of which he was the president of their parish chapter. Discretion seemed the better part of valor in this case, even though he sympathized with many of the nativist arguments on behalf of the colonized Indians. When Professor Hinman elaborated on some aspect of St. Serra's work, John just nodded and bit his tongue in an effort to keep the peace between father and son. He knew he could not resolve the generational tension that strained their relationship since John was in high school. Walter put on his reading glasses and became particularly interested in a new book on display about Serra's life in Spain, Mexico, and California, that included his distinguished academic career before he embarked on the mission field in the New World. When John saw how intrigued his father was with the book, he insisted on buying a copy for him as a gift, in reciprocity for the beautiful pillow his mother had embroidered for them. When they sat down in the café, the professor paged through his new book, pausing to read some of the captions below the pictures and maps generously illustrating the life's work of the saint. Walter sipped his coffee and took a few bites of the flaky churro that John had purchased for them, though he was more interested in the book. John was pleased that he could provide his persnickety father with a pleasant afternoon of Catholic history in America involving the saint he so admired. The book was a king of peace offering, he thought, an olive branch in reparation for the many disagreements that had distanced them from each other over the past several years.

Meanwhile, the ladies were getting along famously, almost like mother and daughter. Walking past the storefronts at the mall, Virginia and Sky admired the dresses, jeans, purses, and shoes displayed in the boutique windows. When they came to the bridal boutique, Virginia remarked about how beautiful she thought Sky would look in the formal wedding gown and long, lace veil that was featured in the window. Sky blushed at the suggestion of going in and looking around, until after they were engaged because, she said, "You know how men are, even your son, afraid of commitment." Their complicit laughter further sealed their feminine bond across the generations. Eventually, they stopped at a little café and sat on the patio. Sky suggested they have a fruit smoothie with a light pastry, so as not to spoil their appetites for supper. Virginia admired her sensible discipline and remarked: "So, that's how you keep your trim figure." While they enjoyed the little respite from window shopping, Virginia asked about her family. Sky told her that her father and baby sister lived in Diablo, in the foothills outside of San Francisco, ever since her mother had died of cancer when Sky was in high school. And it was this essential piece of information that Virginia needed to complete the portrait of the delicate young woman sitting across the café table who would be, hopefully, someday, her daughter-in-law. Virginia immediately apprehended why they seemed to mesh so effortlessly, the one missing the maternal care and affection, the other hoping to find the future spouse for her youngest son. When they finished their break and got up from the patio table, Virginia had it in her mind to dote on Sky as a sign of her growing affection. Seeing the department store name emblazoned above the entrance, she coaxed Sky to try something a little extravagant: "Let's go to Nordstrom's."

Browsing through the women's apparel department, Virginia led Sky to a display of beautiful, designer dresses, one more stylish than the next. While Sky was hesitant to indulge her interest in the chic designs and fabrics once she saw the prices, Virginia helped her overcome her reluctance by reminding her that it was a gift that she wanted her to have as a memento of their visit. "It's as much for him as it is for you," she reassured the younger woman, who was not accustomed to spending several hundred dollars for one article of clothing. "You'll be stunning in that," Virginia proclaimed once Sky had chosen an elegant black cocktail dress with thin straps at the shoulders. "Make sure you're wearing this when he proposes," she said, causing them both to giggle like school girls. "Go try it on, dear." Delighted with her selection, Sky quickly changed in the dressing room and came out to model the fit for John's mother and the saleswoman who came over to assist them. "You're a perfect two," the saleswoman said. "It doesn't need any alterations." Sky turned in front of the long mirror to admire her new dress from every angle. "I have the perfect heels for this," she said excitedly. "We'll take it," Virginia said and reached into her purse for her credit card. Before they left the mall, Virginia bought Sky a colorful silk scarf, to complement the dress, at one of the specialty boutiques.

On the drive home, they tried to talk about other things such as her job in the Sorrento Valley or John's promotion, but, try as they might, they always came back to the dress.

"I've never had anything that expensive," Sky said, self-consciously, though obviously thrilled.

"You deserve it, dear," Virginia reassured the young woman. "I'm so happy that you found the perfect dress. You heard the saleswoman—it was made for you."

The ladies continued to talk about where she might wear it and how John would be delighted to see her in it. Their shopping trip had been a great success on a few different levels, but none so important as the purchase of her designer, black, cocktail dress. Their men would never understand. Sky thanked Virginia profusely all the way back to the duplex.

John and Walter had returned first. While Walter immediately started reading the new book, John busied himself with setting the table for their supper, both men avoiding much discussion about the displays at the museum for fear that it might lead to a debate. On the ride home, the father and son nearly lapsed into their adversarial postures when Walter began expounding on the numerous official recognitions that Saint Junipero Serra had received from the governments of California and the United States over the years, such as the state holiday on the anniversary of his birth, his statue in Washington, D.C., the naming of a freeway in his honor, and the stamp issued by the U.S. Postal Service just a few years ago. The catalogue of secular honors that the professor enumerated almost seemed like a provocation, daring his son to discount these official recognitions since he held little regard for the Church's beatification and canonization of the saint. And the younger man had almost taken the bait, barely restraining himself from saying what was on his mind: that the list of secular honors only reinforced the nativist argument that Junipero Serra was accustomed to collaborating with civil authorities and, therefore, was co-opted by them in the colonization of the Native Americans. Fortunately for the two of them, the inevitable afternoon traffic caused enough of a diversion to change the subject before they could further articulate their conflicting opinions.

When Sky and Virginia returned from their shopping spree, they sensed the tension in the air. The women quickly greeted their men with a kiss to diffuse whatever had trans- pired between father and son. Sky put her packages in their bedroom. Virginia feigned interest in her husband's book, momentarily, then recounted the wonderful day they had together at the mall, careful not to mention the price of the dress she had bought for Sky; she would deal with that back in

Cleveland. Sky returned to the kitchen after having changed into her jeans and a colorful blouse, to prepare their supper. Virginia joined her, further consolidating their confederation in the hope of extending peace over a hearty supper, as she had learned that the Hinman men could be easily distracted with a good meal. Sky checked on the lentil soup that had been stewing in the slow cooker while they were out. She asked Virginia to take a taste, to which she suggested they add a little more salt to please Walter's palate. Sky tied her apron around Virginia to protect her blue dress. While Sky seasoned and stirred the hot soup, Virginia took to cutting the fresh bread into thick slices. Trying to be helpful, John brought the butter to the table and filled their glasses with cold, filtered water, adding a slice of lemon to each glass. Walter took his seat.

Sky ladled the steaming lentil soup from the slow cooker into the large ceramic bowl that she used for such meals. Then she set it in the middle of the table for all to enjoy. She was proud of her recipe and anxious for John's parents to enjoy it. Virginia brought the sliced bread on the cutting board to the table to complement the soup.

Walter cleared his throat, signaling his intention to pray before their super. Again, John and Sky simply bowed their heads while his parents recited the traditional, Catholic prayer of thanksgiving, crossing themselves when they finished.

Sky began serving her soup with the large ladle, starting with Virginia and Walter and then, John, and finally herself. She filled the bowls to the brim, confident in her special dish. John passed her homemade bread around the table with the butter. Within a few minutes, they became quiet, enjoying the delicious soup with each spoonful. The lentils, vegetables, and broth were particularly savory as they had stewed in the slow cooker for longer than usual.

Virginia was the first to compliment Sky on her soup, with Walter following his wife's lead. John mentioned that lentils were common in the diet of the ancient Middle East, trying to establish some vague, biblical credibility for Sky's soup. But the lentil soup was so deli- cious that it needed no bonafides. When Walter asked for a second helping, Sky knew that this supper with John's parents was the success she had hoped for. Virginia did not hesitate to dip her buttered bread into her bowl of rich broth. John had a second bowl, also. The ladies had more, too, but only one ladle each, filling half their bowls.

The wonderful meal enabled their dinner conversation to advance effortlessly, as they talked about their excursions like a typical family home from their day's labor. Sky could not have been more pleased with the impression she was making on John's parents; she wanted them to know that she could take good care of their son.

"So, what did you buy?" John asked Sky.

"Oh, something," Sky said coyly.

"It's a surprise," Virginia said. "You'll see it soon enough. It's a gift from Walter and I."

"Mom, you didn't have to do that," John said.

"I know I didn't have to," she said. "I wanted to. I love this girl."

The word 'love' hung in the air for a moment, hovering over their table like a prophecy.

"Your mother is so kind," Sky said, blushing, not hesitant to voice her affection for Virginia.

"Well, whatever it is," Walter added, "I'm sure you'll look great in it, all dolled up, if I know Ginnie."

Virginia began clearing the soup bowls from the table as Sky brought the fresh fruit platter from the refrigerator. John set out a tray of chocolates to add something sweet for their dessert.

"Don't tell me you made these, too," Virginia said.

"They are homemade, but not by me," Sky said. "Our neighbor, Lucille gives us some whenever she makes a batch. There's nuts, caramels, and cherries. They're scrump- tious."

While the four of them leisurely picked at the grapes, figs, strawberries, and pear slices on the platter, and sampled the rich, homemade chocolates, they seemed to relax into a kind of familiarity that augured well for the whole weekend. They were getting along despite their differences, thanks, in no small part, to the peacemaking efforts of Virginia and Sky.

"While we were at the museum," John said, "I picked up a church bulletin for the Sunday masses at the Mission. There's a noon Mass tomorrow that should give us time for breakfast in the morning and for sight seeing in the afternoon."

"We can go down to the ocean," Sky added. "There are some charming outdoor cafés overlooking the bay."

"That sounds great," Virginia said.

"Thanks, John," Walter said, surprised at his son's thoughtfulness in securing the time for Sunday Mass, since he knew John and Sky were not church goers.

John brought out a bottle of hazelnut liqueur and poured them all a taste in the small cordial glasses that they had for just such occasions. As the evening wound down, the couples were noticeably pleased that they were all getting along so well, especially Walter and John. Their conversation was light and friendly, even entertaining, as Professor Hinman regaled them with some stories about his students and departmental politics, reveiling a charm and wit that endeared him to Sky and surprised his son. The genuine laughter that ensued at the evening table was like a balm that soothed any tensions that may have surfaced over the past couple of days. Virginia sensed that this was the perfect way to end the night and suggested that it was time for 'the old folks' to go to bed. Her timing was impeccable.

So, as John began helping Sky clear the table, she insisted that Virginia and Walter get a good night's rest and leave the clean up to them. Walter was happy to retire and he and his wife shuffled off to their bedroom, but not before Virginia had another chance to kiss and hug her son and his girlfriend.

Once the table was cleared and the bowls, plates, glasses, and utensils stacked in the sink, Sky began to rinse them and place them in the dishwasher, while John put away the leftovers. They did this in a sort of synchronized way while expressing their joy that the evening with his parents had ended on such a high note. When they completed the domes- tic chore, they shut off the lights and went to their bedroom, anxious to find comfort in each other's arms.

With the couples sound asleep, there settled a kind of peace in their duplex, a still- ness that promised hope for the next day, a hush that suggested that the visit of his parents over the weekend had accomplished a deep healing beyond John's wildest imagining, even in his dreams.

When Sky woke up on Sunday morning, a little groggy from the liqueur to which she was not accustomed, she found Virginia, in her robe and slippers, already in the kitchen, rustling about in the refrigerator.

"Good morning, dear," Virginia said as she turned, holding a tupperware container in her hand. "I hope you don't mind. I thought I'd whip up a western omelet for all of us. The peppers and onions are already cut from yesterday. Can I use these mushrooms?" She held out the plastic container.

"Of course," Sky said. "And there's some white cheddar cheese we picked up at the farm." She was pleased that John's mother felt comfortable enough to help her prepare their breakfast.

"I may not know much about California," Virginia said. "But if I know my husband and son, they'll wake up looking for something to eat."

"That's one of John's favorites," Sky said and began cutting a couple of potatoes to complement her omelet.

"I know," Virginia said. "Walter's too, but I usually cube some ham for him with his eggs."

"I'm sorry, but we don't have any," Sky said.

"Don't worry about it, dear," Virginia said. "I've been trying to get Walter to watch his cholesterol, anyhow. The cheese will do fine."

So, the two of them worked side by side at the kitchen counter, gathering the eggs, butter, and cheese to go along with the vegetables. Sky set out the bread. She cut the white cheddar into thin slices so that it would melt more easily in the omelet. While Sky put on the coffee, Virginia began to set the table, familiar enough, after a couple of days, to know where she kept her tableware. The women enjoyed having a partner in the kitchen, as their men were not much help with cooking.

"John should be up, soon," Sky said.

"As soon as Walter smells the coffee," Virginia said, "he'll come shuffling into the kitchen. Men are nothing if not predictable, dear."

Again, the innocent, complicit chuckling.

Sure enough, after a few minutes, Walter and John joined them in the kitchen. While Sky poured the coffee and orange juice, Virginia announced the breakfast menu, which included the fresh raspberry preserves that Sky had purchased at the farm.

"You should come more often," John said to his father, in a humorous allusion to the meals they were enjoying, as well as a veiled expression of gratitude for their visit.

"You seem to be doing well enough," Walter said and sipped his black coffee. "She's some cook," he whispered across the table, just loud enough for the women to hear.

Virginia began sautéing the seasoned peppers, onions, and mushrooms with butter in the large skillet Sky had set on the stove, while Sky started to fry the potatoes. When Virginia began to whisk the half-dozen eggs in a bowl, Sky put four slices of her homemade bread in the toaster. Virginia poured the eggs over the vegetables, added some salt and pepper, then secured the lid on the pan to help the omelet steam. After a couple of minutes, she added the thin slices of cheese that Sky had cut for her. Sky seasoned the potatoes in the pan and watched as Virginia neatly quartered the omelet in the skillet with the edge of the spatula and then skillfully flipped the four portions with a deft turn of her wrist. She brought over the platter for Virginia, then buttered the toast that had popped up. She put the toast and some cut fruit on plates, and the fried potatoes in a serving bowl with a large spoon. The women set out the savory breakfast on the kitchen table with a kind of domestic pride at serving their family this collaborative meal.

Everyone enjoyed the breakfast, especially Walter and John. The friendly conver- sation included mention of the quality of the fresh fruit, sweeter and juicier than what they get back east. Within the hour, their plates were empty and they all seemed pleasantly satisfied. Virginia and Sky smiled and gave each other a little nod.

"Well," John said, "Mass is not until noon, so we all have time to shower and change. The Mission Church is an easy ride on Sunday."

"Why don't you and Walter get yourselves ready," Virginia said. "Sky and I will clean up in here." She wanted some time alone with John's girlfriend to tell her how pleased she was with how things were going between their men.

"Sounds good to me," Walter said and got up from the table, happy to avoid any kitchen duty.

"Thanks, Mom," John said, taking a last gulp of coffee.

"Sky fried the potatoes, you know," Virginia said.

Once the men retired to their rooms to get ready for Mass, the women took the opportunity to confer.

"I was hoping the two of them would get along," Virginia said. "The last time they were together, they got into a big fight."

"What did they argue about?" Sky asked, as she began placing the plates and utensils in the dishwasher.

"I don't even remember," Virginia said while scouring the frying pans. "They've been at it since John was in high school and began disagreeing with the professor."

As they cleared the table, they talked about what else they might do to maintain the peace between father and son.

"After we go to Church," Sky suggested, "we can take a ride to the bay—it's so beautiful and calming."

"That's a great idea, dear," Virginia said. "They can't disagree about the ocean."

When they finished in the kitchen, Virginia gave Sky an affectionate hug. "You're so good for John; I hope you two get married sooner rather than later."

"Me, too," Sky said. "I really love your son. You raised a good man."

The ladies went to their rooms to shower, prepare, and change for the day's outing at Church and the bay. They took ample time to look their best.

On the drive to Church, Walter told a story about John's walk-off homerun in a high school baseball game when he was a junior. It was a victory that led to the section championship. Walter recalled the feat to extol his son to Sky, as well as to express his paternal pride to John. He was making an effort to extend an olive branch to his son.

"You never told me about that," Sky said.

"Oh, he's too modest," Virginia said. "He was quite the athlete."

"He was a good baseball player," Walter added.

John blushed at the praise, but it meant a lot to him coming from his father. Then, he signaled to switch lanes in the light freeway traffic, for the exit to the Mission San Diego. The had made good time and were early for the noon Mass. John parked the car as close to the church as he could, trying to shorten the walk for his parents.

Before they entered the church, they stopped to admire the white adobe building with it towering campanario housing the five large bells.

"This first mission was moved a couple of times," Walter explained to the others, "from its original location overlooking the bay. It was reconstructed a few times, too." It did not take him long to fall into his professorial mode from his reading of the new book.

"What's that big tower with the bells?" Sky asked.

"The bells rang to call the Indians from the fields to Mass," Walter said. "Back in the day, the Mission had thousands of acres of farmland and grazing fields."

John knew most of the history of the Mission, but let his father have the rostrum. He had never brought Sky to this church, or any church, because he had become ambivalent toward his Catholic faith over the years.

The couples walked arm in arm into the church along with several others. Sky watched Walter and Virginia dip their fingers into the small, holy water font and bless themselves as they entered the nave. All of this was unfamiliar to her, yet intriguing.

They took a pew close to the sanctuary, with Walter and Virginia genuflecting in the aisle toward the tabernacle before they took their seats. Uncertain of what to do, Sky followed John's lead and simply slid into the pew. While she had been in a few Protestant churches over the years and was familiar with simple Christian symbols like the cross, she had never been in the more ornate Catholic churches, with their colorful statues and stations, their elaborate sanctuaries and imposing crucifixes. Sky took notice of the vaulted ceiling with its paintings of angels amidst the clouds, suggesting heaven.

The Mass itself was foreign to Sky, with its dialogical prayers, priestly gestures, and congregational postures, with the corresponding chants and hymns. The readings reminded her of the few Protestant services she had attended, but there was something about the solemnity that was appealing to her gentle nature. In his homily, the priest, in green vestments, gave a passionate defense of the missionary zeal of Saint Junipero Serra, who built this first of the California missions two-hundred-fifty years ago. Through the Offertory and the priest's Eucharistic Prayer, Sky became distracted and found herself studying the art forms that adorned the walls and ceiling, the sanctuary and floor tiles. The consecratory bells brought her back to the prayer, momentarily. When it came time for communion, she stayed in the pew with John, while Virginia and Walter joined the other communicants walking toward the priest distributing the hosts. When they returned to their pew, she noticed how absorbed in prayer they were for several minutes. The closing hymn was in Spanish, its celebratory rhythm appealing to Sky. All in all, her first experience of a Catholic Mass was a good one, if unfamiliar.

On the drive to the Bay of San Diego, Virginia asked Sky what she wanted to do when they got there. Sky told her about their favorite, little coffee shop where they liked to go in the evening to watch the sun set over the Pacific.

John parked the car near the coffee shop and its outdoor tables. They found a vacant table with a great view of the ocean bay. The June sun was hot but Walter and Virginia enjoyed the warmth on their arms and faces.

"This is a little nicer than a stroll along the Cuyahoga," Virginia said to Walter, mesmerized by the beauty of the ocean and sky at the horizon.

"That's the river that runs through Cleveland," John said to Sky. "It's been know to catch fire from the industrial pollution."

"Just a few times," Walter interjected, loosening his tie. "They've been cleaning it up in recent years."

Sky ordered them four, iced green teas with lemon and mint to combat the after- noon heat. The waitress returned to their table promptly with the refreshing drinks.

"This is so beautiful," Virginia remarked. "I can see why you love it so much."

"The ocean breeze keeps things cool," John said. "The weather's near perfect except for a few weeks in the summer."

"I'd miss the seasons," Walter said.

Sipping their iced teas through straws, the four of them fell into a pleasant conver- sation as they looked out on the soothing waters of the bay. They talked about how much they enjoyed the brief visit and the chance to spend quality time together. John ordered another round of iced teas, wanting to linger at the table

205

and not relinquish the scenic view of San Diego Bay. When they finally rose from the table, the four of them were in harmony about the importance of staying in touch with each other in the months ahead.

On the drive back to San Marcos, John put on the radio to hear the weather and news. The newscaster announced another week of perfect weather for San Diego: highs in the eighties, lows in the sixties. Then, a commentator discussed an incident that had occurred in Los Angeles that past week. It seemed that nativist protestors had torn down the statue of Saint Junipero Serra in Serra Park because of his supposed collaboration with the Mexican government in the colonization of Native Americans in the eighteenth century. The news reporter put the incident in context with the other statues that were being toppled across the United States that summer, mostly confederate generals from the Civil War.

"Can you believe that?" Walter declared from the back seat. "A saint of the Church desecrated for some revisionist version of American history—jackasses."

John turned off the radio.

"Now, don't get upset, dear," Virginia said, trying to calm down her husband.

"Don't get upset," Walter responded. "He petitioned the Mexican government for an Indian Bill of Rights to protect them. He built the twenty-one missions to preserve their culture while propagating the faith."

"Some might say the faith of the Europeans," John countered, and then immediately wished that he hadn't said anything.

"Europeans, Americans," Walter shot back. "He was evangelizing in the New World—spreading the gospel of Jesus Christ."

While Sky understood the general disagreement about the interpretation of Saint Serra's work among the Indians, the more subtle nuances of collaboration or evangelization were unfamiliar to her. Virginia could see where this was going and tried to change the subject.

"So, what have you planned for our Sunday supper, Sky?" she asked, hoping to interest the men before they got into a heated argument.

"Angel hair pasta with tuna fish and capers in a light tomato-basil sauce," Sky explained, picking up on Virginia's redirection of the conversation. "It's one of our favorites."

Walter was mumbling something in the backseat about the Bolsheviks tearing down statues in Russia a hundred years ago.

John was glad when he pulled into his parking space at the duplex. He was hoping to avoid a debate with his father.

Once inside the house, Walter asked John to find a local news feed on the internet which was set up in the living room. Reluctantly, John found a site featuring news from Los Angeles. Within a few minutes, Virginia and Sky, in the kitchen, could hear Walter talking out loud as the toppling of the Serra statue was being amplified by a panel of experts in Church history, Native American heritage, and public policy. John excused himself to go to the bathroom.

While the ladies worked together to prepare the mid-afternoon supper, Walter was seething in the living room the more he watched the panel discussion. He looked for his son to engage in debate, but John was shrewdly keeping his distance from his enraged father. When he finally returned to the living room, John suggested they go for a walk in the nearby park 'on this beautiful day,' trying to pry Walter from the computer. But his father was focused on the various points of view expressed by the panel of experts. He continued mumbling in defense of the saint when one of the panelists advanced a harsh criticism of his work among the American Indians.

Meanwhile, Sky and Virginia cooperated on another meal for the four of them. John offered to set the table, more to stay away from his father than to be hospitable. Sky took all the ingredients out of the refrigerator and the panty cupboard: the box of angel hair pasta, the olive oil, the jar of capers, the balsamic vinegar, the jar of tomato sauce, the fresh basil, the minced garlic, the grated cheese, and the jar of artichoke hearts. She asked Virginia to slice some of her homemade bread.

"This is a simple dish I learned from my neighbor," Sky said. "She said the Italians used the tuna fish in place of meat on Fridays. Do Catholics still have to give up meat on Friday?"

"Only during Lent, dear," Virginia explained the Church's current dietary restrictions to Sky. "I never thought to use tuna fish in my sauce."

"Can you make the dressing for the artichoke salad?" Sky asked her. "Oil, balsamic, salt and pepper."

While the women skillfully prepared the simple, Sunday supper, John returned to the living room to join his father, determined not to get into an argument about the toppling of the statue. The professor was still watching the panel discussion on the internet.

"Listen to these idiots," Walter said in exasperation. "It's like they don't believe in history."

"It's just a different interpretation of history, Dad," John said, trying to calm his father down.

"Don't give me that," Walter said, running his hand over his thick head of hair. "I doubt that one ever read a book." He pointed to the panelist on the far left, both literally and figuratively, of the screen.

"Well, there are some educated people leading the nativist cause and calling for land reparations," John said, attempting to counter his father's ad hominem assertions.

"Yeah, educated at Berkley, or some other leftist institution," Walter said.

"Sky graduated from Berkley," John said, insulted as his father's condemnation of the West Coast's equivalent of an Ivy League university.

"Well, she's sensible," Walter said, "unlike these nincompoops. They distort reality to fit their ideology."

From the kitchen, Virginia could hear the faised voices of her husband and son. She quickly finished tossing the artichoke salad and placed it on the table next to the bread and butter.

"It's time for supper," she called into the living room where the men were sparring. Sky set the large bowl of steaming tuna fish pasta in the center of the table and then filled their water glasses.

When John came to the table, he suggested they have some Chardonnay wine with their last supper together. He got the bottle of Chardonnay from the refrigerator, while Sky set out the wine glasses.

"This is a good California wine," John said while he poured. "Not too dry and reasonably priced."

"I could use a drink after what I was listening to," Walter said. "Let's pray."

After leading the table in the traditional, Catholic prayer before meals, he could not help himself from adding a petition about the preservation of the memory of the saintly Serra.

John made a toast to his parents for making the long, cross-county visit. They all clinked their glasses of wine.

"It's been so enjoyable meeting you," Sky said. "I hope you like the pasta."

"It smells wonderful," Virginia said.

Walter was still brooding about the newscast. The tension he generated at the table was nearly palpable.

Sky served the angel hair in generous portions on their plates, careful that everyone got ample tuna fish, sauce, and capers.

"I've learned two new dishes from Sky on this trip," Virginia said, taking another opportunity to compliment John's girlfriend, "the lentil soup and this tuna fish pasta."

After a couple of mouthfuls of the angel hair, Walter managed to say he thought it was 'very good.' Then, he took a full gulp of the chilled wine.

John passed the homemade bread and rich butter to his father as a kind of peace offering, hoping that the meal might assuage Walter's offended sensibilities.

And, for a while, Walter managed to suppress his anger at the toppling of the saint's statue in Los Angeles, mindful of his table manners. But with a second glass of wine, he could not restrain himself from interrupting their quiet supper. While the food was delicious, the news was distasteful.

"I just can't get over the stupidity of those thoughtless rabble-rousers toppling his statue," he said. "The Indians themselves celebrated the legacy of Serra when they erected those monuments."

"Did they have a choice?" John said, against his better judgement." They were a conquered people."

Virginia sensed that the tension was ready to disrupt Sky's peaceful supper table. "Did you try the artichokes, Walter?" she said, passing the salad bowl. "I mixed the dressing myself."

After his father took some of the artichokes, John saw that his plate was empty, so he offered him more of the tasty pasta.

"Just a small one," Walter said and raised his plate.

Sky was delighted that John's parents were enjoying the vegetarian meal she had prepared for them.

"If it wasn't for Saint Junipero," Walter said between bites, "the Indians could've starved after the Spaniards took their lands. He protected the young, Indian women from the soldiers, too."

John had had about enough of his father's pontificating about early American history. He could hardly remain silent anymore.

"Those capers add just the right bite to this mild dish, dear," Virginia said to Sky, trying to move their dinner conversation away from that bone of contention.

"Thank you," Sky said to Virginia, who, with another compliment, was growing ever more endeared to her.

"And another thing, John," Walter added when he finished a last forkful of the artichoke salad. "For the next twenty years until his death, Padre Serra established the other twenty missions as safe havens for the Indians along the coast of California all the way up to San Francisco."

"And a hundred years later," John answered his father, "the mission lands were reduced to a few acres and the Indian populations were decimated by European diseases against which they had no immunities."

"You can't blame the secularization of the missions on Junipero Serra," Walter countered. "He was long dead by the time the Mexican government took them over."

"That's the point," John said, straightening up in his chair. "He enabled the further confiscation of their lands in the next century by herding them into those mission colonies and domesticating a proud native people."

"You can't blame him for what the governments of Mexico, and then the United States, did after his death," Walter said, taking another gulp of wine. "You're taking his life's work out of its historical context. I taught you better than that, son."

"You taught me how to think critically," John said, accidently knocking over his wine glass with a wave of his arm. "And I won't acquiesce just because the church and state declare him a hero."

By now, the ladies knew that they had lost this round. Their men were at it.

"What is it with you?" Walter said rhetorically. "You're still fighting against authority like you did when you were a teenager. Grow up!"

"Grow up!" John said, raising his voice and standing at the table. "I am. I won't be bullied by a professor desperate to preserve the reputation of his beloved patron saint, especially in my own house."

Virginia knew that they had crossed the line; there was no turning back, now.

Sky refrained from offering them dessert and coffee.

"Well, then," Walter said. "Maybe it's time for us to go if we're not welcomed here."

"Well, maybe it is," John said, and as soon as he said it, looked at his mother, apologetically.

Walter got up from the table and threw his napkin down on his plate. He stomped off to their bedroom, grumbling.

Sky was on the brink of tears. The supper she had hoped would seal their familial bond had turned into a fiasco. Virginia saw how upset she was and went over to give her a hug. She shot her son a stern look, and he left the duplex to walk it off, mumbling an apology as he went out of the front door.

"It's not your fault, dear," Virginia whispered to Sky. "You did everything you could to create a peaceful, family atmosphere. Sometimes men are just hellbent on fighting. It's in their DNA," she said in her comforting, maternal voice.

"I wanted everything..." she couldn't finish her thought.

"Don't worry, dear," Virginia patted her back. "They've been doing this for the past decade."

"But we were having such a good time," Sky managed to say between sniffles.

"I know," Virginia said.

For the rest of the evening, the two women diplomatically worked on their men to move them toward a truce. They used their arsenal of feminine wiles to calm them down without aggravating the situation.

The next morning, though Walter and John just nodded their 'farewell' and avoided shaking hands at the airport, Virginia kissed her son 'good-bye' and embraced Sky warmly. Virginia squeezed her hand as she kissed her cheek, exuding some ancient wisdom more sublime than history. "We'll find a way, dear," she whispered, bringing a smile to Sky's face, because the women knew.

Honeymoon

Oahu

During the long flight from Los Angeles to Hawaii, Kate had tried to sleep a couple of times, but now, with her arm laced around Tim's, she finally fell into a quiet slumber, her head resting on his shoulder. Tim was awake, enjoying the sensation of his wife nestling beside him as they approached the destination of their honeymoon.

He recalled how he had carried her across the threshold of their home after the wedding reception, proud that he had completed the remodeling of the old house in time for their first nights together as husband and wife. Though the house was in a gentrified neighborhood of inner city Syracuse, Kate had already begun to make their new home warm and comfortable with the plush green carpeting and colorful floral draperies she chose, the wooden cabinetry she selected for the kitchen, and the fragrant red, white, and purple petunias with the trumpet- shaped petals she planted in their small backyard along the cyclone fence between their property and their next door neighbors.' Their neighbors, an elderly couple who had lived in their house for more than forty years, had raised their four children in this neighborhood, and seemed delighted to have a nice young couple moving in next to them.

As the plane made its descent over the Pacific Ocean, approaching the islands, Tim's ears popped with the changing air pressure and Kate stirred beside him. In her sleep, Kate had dreamt about how beautiful their wedding Mass at St. Joseph's had been, how perfect the ceremony had proceeded, beginning with her father walking her down the aisle in her traditional white wedding dress with the long, lace train, her three sisters in their bridesmaids' gowns beside her near the altar, their long, blond hair fashionably coiffed, their salon nails a pastel blue to match their dresses. In her dreaming, she could almost feel her mother's tears on her face when they embraced at the sign of peace.

"Are we there yet?" she mumbled as she straightened up in her seat, still drowsy from her doze and relishing the remnant of her dream.

"You better fasten your seat belt, babe," Tim said.

She squeezed his muscular arm, pleased that he was so solicitous of her.

"Did you remember the rental car?" Kate asked Tim, checking on a planning detail that he, unlike her, might have forgotten.

"Don't worry," Tim said. "It'll be waiting for us at the airport."

Kate was one of those brides who had meticulously planned every detail of their wedding and reception, keeping the paperwork and notes in a special, white binder. But she had left the honeymoon preparations to Tim, the flight plans and hotel reservations, the tours and sightseeing, hopeful that he would follow through on all the details. So far, so good, she thought.

After loading their luggage into the trunk of the grey Nissan Altima sedan, Tim drove the half-hour, or so, from the Oahu International Airport to their hotel. Kate was wide-eyed, looking first at the people in their colorful clothes, then the shanty houses in the depressed area beyond the airport, the rows of military housing, and, finally, at the tall palm trees lining the highway. The ocean was on Tim's side and he was mesmerized by the undulating waters and the bright blue sky at the horizon.

"We're here," he said, reaching over to touch Kate's hand.

"I can't believe we made it," Kate said. "I've always dreamt about a honeymoon in Hawaii."

"I love you, honey," Tim said as he squeezed her hand.

"I love you, too," Kate said, raising his hand to her lips for a gentle kiss.

Though they were both anxious to begin their Hawaiian honeymoon, the long flights to Los Angeles and then Oahu were catching up with them, and so they both were looking forward to some rest once they arrived at the hotel. After all, they would have eight days to explore the islands and each other.

Kate, a nurse, had grown up with the stories of Mother Marianne Cope and the Franciscan sisters from Syracuse who had accompanied her to Hawaii in the eighteen-eighties to help Fr. Damien de Veuster care for the lepers on Molokai. In the months before her wedding, she found time to read her mother's worn copy of Saint Marianne's biography and had her heart set on making the pilgrimage to the shrine at the former leper colony. Her mother, who volunteered in the gift shop at the Syracuse convent, had urged her not to miss the opportunity to visit the historic shrine while on their honeymoon. Kate had been fascinated by the heroic compassion of Mother Marianne and her nuns ever since she first heard the stories when she was a little girl. In fact, the Franciscan saint had inspired her life's work as a nurse.

Ever since Kate had first suggested Hawaii for their honeymoon, Tim had become excited with the prospect of hiking up one of the inactive volcanoes to peer into its fathomless crater. At the University of Buffalo, he had been a geology major and briefly considered graduate studies until, upon graduation, he followed his brothers and cousins, his father and grandfather, to the Syracuse Fire Department. He made the choice to battle elemental forces rather than study them. The Hawaiian islands chain had been formed by a series of volcanoes, now primarily dormant, over several millennia; they were a geologist's dream. So, while planning their itinerary, he penciled in the volcano hike on Maui, where they would be staying for a few days during their honeymoon.

As the Gallaghers approached the concierge's desk at the Sheraton Waikiki Hotel, a smiling, young Polynesian woman greeted them with an 'Aloha' and placed colorful leis around their necks. Kate touched the fresh flowers and inhaled their sweet fragrance as they rode up in the elevator. The porter brought their luggage to the seventh floor honeymoon suite and Tim tipped him generously. With the door locked, they began undressing: Kate laying her light- weight, floral dress on the divan at the foot of the bed and removing her bra, Tim tossing his white shirt and slacks across the luggage, pulling off his socks. It felt good for the newlyweds to kick off their shoes.

Kate plopped down on the large bed atop the covers. Tim snuggled behind his wife, draping his arm around her. He gently kissed her bare shoulder.

"Nevermind, Romeo," she said, giggling at another of his incessant gestures of affection, though she loved feeling so desired in his strong embrace.

"I guess I'm a little tired, too," Tim said, perceiving from her playful tone that his wife wanted to sleep, for now.

Within a few minutes, the newlyweds were sound asleep on the comfortable bed in the large, bright suite Tim had reserved for the first few days of their honeymoon.

When Kate awoke a couple of hours after they had fallen asleep, Tim was still snoring, so she wriggled out of his arms as deftly as she could, trying not to wake him. She put on the white, terry cloth hotel robe, and then sat in the plush chair facing the picture window, peering off toward the horizon where the sky and sea met beyond the tall buildings of Oahu. She ate a couple pieces of sweet pineapple from the colorful fruit basket on the cocktail table. After a few minutes she got up and went into the spacious bathroom to take a refreshing shower.

The sound of the shower woke Tim, but he was in no hurry to get up. He was still drowsy, feeling the jet lag of the flights from Syracuse to Chicago, from Chicago to Los Angeles, from Los Angeles to Oahu. Lying on their hotel bed, he realized that he was embarking on a much more mysterious journey with Kate than even the exotic Hawaiian islands, a journey that would change his life forever. He loved his beautiful bride more deeply than he had loved anyone in his life. He could sense himself changing, too, calming down, knowing a kind of peace that eluded him through his teenage and college years, and now, finally, in his young adult years, focusing his passion on the woman of his dreams. When he looked into her clear, blue eyes, he saw a reflection of goodness, an innocence and tenderness that drew the best out of him, not only toward her, but also toward everyone around him. She had even awakened the dormant religious sentiment in him that had dissipated since he went to college. Going to church with her on most Sunday mornings these past couple of years had become something that he looked forward to, even though he had been more a nominal Catholic, checking in only on Christmas and Easter, before he had met Kate. His random thoughts were drifting in various directions until, in his mind's eye, he settled on the angelic face of his beloved. Then, he heard her whisper breathe in his ear.

"Tim, honey," Kate said, placing her hand on his chest. "It's time to get up. You have to shower before supper."

He pretended to still be sleeping, then quickly turned and hugged her in her terry cloth robe. He rubbed his scratchy, day-old beard along her smooth cheek and chin, causing her to laugh aloud as she squirmed to get out of his arms.

"Stop that," she giggled when she finally got up from the bed. "C'mon; I'm hungry."

"Me, too," he said with a mischievous grin and reached for her as she slid away.

"Tim," she said. "Please."

"Okay," he said and let go of the cloth belt on her robe that he was clinging to. He could not resist her plaintive voice with its feminine charm. On his way to the bathroom, he picked up a piece of the juicy, yellow mango from the fruit basket.

While he was showering, Kate found her makeup bag amid their luggage and placed his personal hygiene kit on the bathroom sink. She used the hair dryer provided on the wall near the vanity to dry her long, blond hair, and then brushed it into shape. Settling at the vanity, she inspected her face in the mirror. She applied the moisturizer first, followed by the foundation, and lastly, she lightly dusted some blush on her cheeks. She took her time, as Tim had wisely made their dinner reservations for the elegant hotel dining room so they could relax on this first night of their Hawaiian honeymoon. As she carefully applied her eye liner, Kate thought about how wonderful things had been going since their engagement last Christmas and, now, with their wedding and honeymoon. It felt to her as if they had been swept up in a movement larger than themselves, a wave of hope and joy this past year, or so, that was propelling them forward into this new adventure of marriage. Neatly brushing her eye lashes, Kate had to hold back the tears when she recalled how gentle and patient Tim had been with her those first couple of nights together in their home, despite his obvious ardor. She was happy that she had prevailed on him to restrain themselves before they were married, so that their wedding night, and these honeymoon days, could seal the vows they pledged before God at Saint Joseph's. Looking intently into the mirror, she carefully colored her full lips with her favorite rose lipstick. Pausing, she realized how thrilled she was with their tender intimacies, how much she desired to kiss him, how loved she felt in his embrace. She knew, more than ever, that she had found the man she could love for the rest of her life, the man she could give herself to unreservedly. The man who loved her above all others. Though naturally modest, Kate enjoyed the freedom of dressing and undressing in front of her husband, aware that Tim was watching her. The colorful dress with the bright, floral designs that she slipped on, sensuously hugged her trim figure. Before she knew it, Tim was zipping up the dress and, then, embracing her and nuzzling her neck.

"You're beautiful, babe," he whispered between kisses.

"I'll bet you said that to all the girls," Kate teased him as he tightened his embrace.

"But I mean it like never before," Tim protested. "You're the most beautiful woman I have ever seen."

Kate knew that Tim had a reputation of being a 'ladies man' before they started dating. Her sisters and her girlfriends thought he was a real 'catch.' She gave him a light peck on the cheek, not wanting to smear her rose lipstick.

Leaving their suite, they radiated an almost palpable love that was immediately noticeable to anyone who saw them in the hallway, on the elevator, or in the hotel dining room. They were a striking couple in their bright, floral outfits: she in that colorful evening dress and he in his collared, Hawaiian shirt, that she had bought him for the trip, and his neatly pressed khakis. As soon as they sat down at their reserved table, the maitre d' popped open a bottle of champagne and poured the honeymooners a glass each. "Compliments of the house," he said and placed the opened bottle in a bucket of ice on their table.

"Thank you," they said. They clinked their glasses, toasting their marriage, then sipped the sweet, effervescent champagne on this first, formal supper of their honeymoon.

Their waitress recommended the evening's special: fresh ahi tuna sautéed with macadamia nuts, and served with long grain rice and island greens; which they were happy to order. She also suggested some poi, a purple paste made from the taro plant, as an appetizer with fried banana crisps for scooping. Neither of them were familiar with Hawaiian cuisine, so they appreciated her advice with the exotic menu. Melinda, their waitress, smiled with the joy emanating from the honeymoon couple, who touched hands and leaned into each other like lovebirds.

While the food was delicious, Tim and Kate were completely engaged with each other, barely cognizant of the other diners. She was enamored with his charming dinner conversation about the itinerary he had planned for the next few days, while he was enchanted with her exquisite blue eyes and the delicate skin of her face and neck. Even while eating, she seemed the epitome of feminine grace. Somehow, the civility of this first honeymoon supper in the elegant hotel dining room heightened their desire for each other. Melinda discretely kept her interruptions to a minimum, refilling their champagne and water glasses only as needed.

"When do we go to Molokai?" Kate asked Tim as they enjoyed their robust Kona coffee and the colorful platter of island fruits, including guava, mango, papaya, and pineapple.

"That's later this week," Tim said vaguely. "We'll go there from Maui."

Tim signed for the check, charging it to their suite, leaving the friendly Melinda a generous tip.

As they walked through the lobby, Tim kept his arm around Kate's waist; she was feeling the champagne. They kissed in the elevator before getting off on the seventh floor.

That night, and the next few days on Oahu, were a blur of honeymoon passion, ease and typical tourist fun. From lounging in their hotel robes to rising leisurely with the morning sun, from shopping for clothes, jewelry, and knick knacks for their home, to snacking at food trucks, from visiting the historical Pearl Harbor National Park, to exploring the expansive Polynesian Cultural Center, the newlyweds were enamored with each other and with the idyllic tropical islands that they had chosen for their honeymoon. Swimming in the brisk, blue ocean or sun bathing on their beach towels in the warm white sand, they each were delighted with how attractive their spouse appeared: Kate in her colorful, floral, two-piece bathing suit; Tim in his blue boxer trunks. Kate even teased him about hiding behind his sunglasses to sneak a glance when some pretty young women in skimpy bikinis passed by. Even just sightseeing around the island in their rental car was a pleasant adventure: sipping tropical drinks through straws from coconuts, and enjoying a variety of fresh fish tacos or exotic bowls of octopus, greens, and Hawaiian spices. At the hotel's luau on their last night, Kate, in her new sarong and seashell necklace, joined the provocative hula dancers swaying to the pulsing drum beat in the moonlight, both surprising and delighting her husband. At the end of each night, they ended up in each other's arms. Even in the public places they visited during the daytime, Kate relished Tim's constant tenderness, hanging onto his arm as they strolled through the shopping district, blushing when his hand gently caressed her waist. And during these carefree honeymoon days, only once did Kate think to mention Molokai, again, to which Tim reassured her that their pilgrimage to the former leper colony would depart from Maui during their three-day stay on the island, their last days in Hawaii. So far, everything is perfect, she thought.

Maui

The Gallaghers took the early flight to Maui, where they would stay for the last few days of their honeymoon. The island of Maui was less commercial than Oahu, so Tim planned only one main event for each of the three days, which would allow them to wind down from their whirlwind days on Oahu. On the short flight, Tim explained to Kate, again, that they would be going snorkeling on the coral reef after lunch, then hike up Haleakala, the enormous dormant volcano that overshadowed the island, tomorrow, and, then, on Friday, make the pilgrimage to Molokai Island to the shrine of Saints Damien and Marianne. Tim, who kept in good shape because of his work as a fireman, was most excited about the hike up Haleakala because of his interest in geology, while Kate was thrilled with the pilgrimage to the remote Kalaupapa National Park, which housed the shrine at the former leper colony. Kate, too, was in good shape because of her work as a nurse. They were young, healthy, and newly married, ready to face together any challenges the islands might pose.

The plush Intercontinental Hotel that Tim had booked had an elegant ambiance, the brilliant crystal chandelier looming over the lobby. They were met, again, by a friendly, young Polynesian woman who greeted them with an 'Aloha' and a kiss on the cheek as she placed the leis around their necks. The porter followed them in the freight elevator to their third floor honeymoon suite, wheeling their luggage on a cart, including the few extra bags filled with new clothes and souvenirs. When the porter came to their room, Tim tipped him generously, appreciative of his careful handling of their luggage. Kate admired the tropical flower arrangement on the cocktail table with its exotic purple, pink, and orange palette, surrounded by leafy, green palm fronds. She inhaled their pungent fragrance.

"The people have been so friendly on the islands," Kate said once they were alone. "You'd be friendly, too," Tim said, "if you lived in paradise. And besides, being good to the tourists is their bread and butter."

As the couple unpacked, Kate talked about her impression of the Hawaiian people they had met: the demure women with their long, black hair and colorful skirts, some barefoot, and the muscular men in loose, white shirts and sandals, with no body hair. Their complexion was a light, brown color burnished by the sun, and the women wore little makeup, she noted with her nurse's precise habit of observation, their dark eyes naturally sultry and luminous.

"They always seem to be smiling," Kate said, "especially the children."

"Come, here, babe," Tim said as he opened the sliding glass door to their balcony. "You have to see this."

From their balcony, Tim and Kate looked out over the shimmering, blue bay, the waters undulating in an hypnotic rhythm. Tim put his arm around Kate as they peered out over the pristine, sunlit panorama. The cool, morning breeze brushed their faces.

"You know how to pick 'em," he complimented her about her insistence on their honeymoon in Hawaii.

Kate hugged Tim with both of her arms. "One place is more beautiful than the next," she said. "We'll have these memories for the rest of our lives."

Tim turned toward her and gave her a prolonged kiss, his strong arm holding his precious wife to his body.

"I love you, Kate," he whispered near her ear.

"I love you, too, Tim," she answered.

After they finished unpacking their suitcases and making some arrangements in the suite, they ordered a light, room service brunch: croissants, butter, and preserves, coffee, and a small tray of fresh fruit. They did not want to have too much in their stomachs when they went snorkling in a couple of hours. They were in no hurry, so sitting close together on the comfortable couch, they ate their meal in a leisurely manner, taking advantage of this little pause from their frenetic, island activities to chat about their adventures on Oahu. They both felt a kind of sweet contentment, whiling away the time together with teasing and laughter, occasional kisses, and admiring their wedding rings, especially her sparkling diamond.

When they got up after a couple of hours, they changed into their bathing suits and, over them, their shorts, shirts, and sandals. Kate packed a couple of the large, hotel bath towels into her floral, carry-on bag, along with some combs, brushes, and skin cream. In the lobby, Tim asked the concierge to call them a cab, which pulled up in front of the hotel in a few minutes. All the while, Tim, who had done some scuba diving, talked to Kate about the safety of snorkeling in the shallow waters of the coral reef. She felt reassured by her husband's encouragement.

While the small boat set out into the bay, Kate and Tim took off their street clothes. The instructor explained the use of the flippers, mask, and snorkel. There were a few other people going snorkeling that afternoon and they were all visibly excited. On the other side of the boat, two men were donning their scuba gear over their wet suits. When the boat finally anchored, the deckhand gave them a few more instructions and then positioned Kate and Tim and the others at the edge of the boat to slip into the ocean. Nothing could have prepared them for the cold waters this far out into the Pacific. While the snorkelers floated in the waves above the

reef for a few minutes, adjusting to the water temperature and testing their snorkels, Tim noticed the divers
nearby, probably watching for any signs of sharks.

When Kate opened her eyes in the water behind the
glass mask, she was stunned by the brilliant colors and
innumerable fish that darted along the reef. Once she
got used to propelling herself with the flippers and
breathing through the mouthpiece of the snorkel, she
moved gracefully along the pink coral, hundreds of fish
swimming beside her at arm's length. Tim stayed near
her, making sure that she was comfortable in her gear.
He pointed to a larger orange fish out in front of them;
the other fish were of various smaller sizes, some with
spots, some striped. When he took her hand, he positioned himself so that she was between him and the
reef. After a few minutes, when he was confident of her
safety and the ease with which she propelled herself
with the flippers, he let go of her hand so that they
could swim more freely through the dazzling array of
neon-colored fish that thrived along the coral reef. Kate
was enchanted by the panoply of shimmering shapes
and bright colors that swam in, out, and along the pink
reef. She was fascinated by the natural beauty that lived
just below the surface of the ocean, a world as new and
wondrous to her as the new intimacies she shared with
her husband. Swimming with the teeming schools of
fish, she lost all sense of time, so that she was surprised
when one of the divers caught up with their group to

signal that it was time to return to the boat. They had been in the clear, cold, magical waters for about an hour, but it seemed longer due to the overwhelming effect on her senses.

As soon as they were back in their hotel room and took off their damp clothing, they felt a passionate desire for each other, the exhilarating effect of their snorkeling adventure. Afterwards, they lay in each other's arms and fell into a euphoric doze. When Kate opened her eyes an hour later, she was facing Tim's broad back. She saw, again, the scar that he got from rescuing that little girl in the house fire. She traced her finger along the red scar from his neck up into his scalp along the back of his head. Then she softly kissed the scar on his neck.

When Kate got out of bed, she went to the bathroom to shower off the residue of the sea salt in her hair and on her skin. Hearing the shower, Tim woke up. As he lay in bed, he remembered to check on their departure time for the hike up the Haleakala Volcano tomorrow morning. He got up and retrieved the notebook that he used to keep the telephone and e-mail numbers of their honeymoon itinerary from the pocket of his suitcase. He thought that their departure at the base of the volcano was scheduled for six on Thursday morning, but he wanted to call to confirm the plans he had made months ago. He was right, they would begin their hike with a party of a dozen at six a.m. He figured that they could get their taxi-cab about five-thirty, He planned on a good meal tonight, then time to pack, and early to bed to prepare themselves for the strenuous hike up Haleakala. When Kate came out of the bathroom in her white terry cloth robe, Tim put on his hotel robe and went toward the bathroom for his shower.

"You smell fresh," he said as they passed each other.

"That shower felt good," she said, drying her hair with a towel. "That shampoo has a tropical scent."

Tim was out of the shower, toweling off, before Kate was dressed. He smiled at the new routine of having to wait for his attractive wife to do her makeup, brush her hair, and complete her look for supper. Women, he thought, can't live with them, can't live without them; he recalled the aphorism that the guys at the firehouse often repeated for his benefit, especially these past few weeks as his wedding day approached.

At supper in the hotel dining room, they were joined by dozens of other vacationers; the room was near full. Tim and Kate talked quietly about the snorkeling outing earlier that day, trying to find the right words to express the beauty and mystery of that underwater wonderland. They sipped the sauvignon blanc that Tim ordered for their meal as the waitress served the plate of steamed mussels and smoked oysters that Kate selected for their appetizer. Squeezing a little, fresh lemon juice on the mussels, Tim mentioned the early departure time for the hike up Haleakala tomorrow. "We should eat some carbs, too, babe; we'll need the energy for the climb," Tim said. "But not too much."

"Yes, Dr. Gallagher," Kate teased him about his dietary instructions. "I know how to eat." "Well, I'm getting the linguine with clam sauce," Tim said, as he surveyed the menu. Then he took a mouthful of the smoked oysters on a thin cracker.

"That sounds good," Kate agreed. "A nice salad, too."

While they enjoyed the savory appetizers and waited for the waitress to bring their salads, Kate noticed the family seated at a table across the dining room. They stood out because most of the room was filled with couples: young like them, middle-aged, and older.

She saw a bassinet sitting on a chair near the mother, who tended to the baby. Her husband and their two other children were busy eating. For the first time on their honeymoon, Kate wondered about the possibility that they might have conceived a baby of their own these past several days since their wedding. Oh, please, God, she prayed silently. She so wanted to be a mother.

The waitress brought their salads and refilled their wine glasses. They enjoyed the island greens, goat cheese, nuts, and exotic fruits tossed together in the fresh salad with a light, sweet dressing.

"So, when do we leave for Molokai on Friday?" Kate asked Tim between bites.

"I'll check when we get back to our room," Tim said.

"Don't you have it on your phone?" Kate said.

"No, I prefer paper," Tim said. "I'll check when we get back to our room. But it will be early, too, because we have to catch the flight and then hike down the big hill to the Kalaupapa National Park where the shrine is."

When the waitress brought their entrees, they both dived into the linguini, relishing the white clam sauce with every forkful. The afternoon's snorkeling and their romantic interlude afterwards had given them both quite an appetite. While she sopped up the clam sauce with a piece of sweet, Hawaiian bread, Kate noticed the family getting up from their table, the mother securing the bassinet on her arm.

Kate and Tim had a fresh fruit platter for dessert with a cup of rich Kona coffee. When the waitress came around to refill their cups, Kate turned away her offer, not wanting too much caffeine in their systems lest it disrupt their sleep. She knew they had to get up before sunrise. "Tim," Kate said between bites of the sweet pineapple, "Tell me, again, how you got that scar on your neck and scalp."

"You know," Tim said, sipping his coffee. "I told you before."

"But I want to hear you tell the story, again" she insisted.

"Well, okay," he started. "It was a big house fire on the North Side. We thought we got everybody out, but then the mother was hysterical because she couldn't find her little Sophia among her children wrapped in blankets nearby."

"Sophia," Kate whispered her name.

"So, I put my helmet back on, affixed my mask and gloves, then turned toward the house," Tim continued. "Before I entered, I heard the mother and the other children shout:

'Second floor.'"

Kate was listening intently to Tim's recounting of the rescue.

"The adrenalin was pumping through my body as I ran up the stairs. The flames had consumed the wooden railing; I couldn't grab it. I heard a faint crying when I reached the landing and I followed the child's voice through the thick smoke. I could barely see the doorway; I had to wipe the soot from my mask. I heard the crying and, with one hand along the wall, located the little girl hiding under a blanket behind a metal cabinet. I had my gloves on, so I pushed it aside. I scooped up the little girl in the blanket and ran out of the room and down the stairs. The fire was blazing hot and I felt something on my neck," he recalled. "But before I knew it, we were outside, clear of the house, coughing from the smoke. Sophia's mother gathered the little girl in her arms, both of them crying. She must've said 'Thank you!' a hundred times. One of the guys doused me with the fire hose." Kate's eyes misted with tears.

"Well, I had been on the department for a few years back then, but I made a rookie mistake," Tim said, pausing to take another sip of coffee. "In my haste, I forgot to flip up my hood before I grabbed my helmet. That's how my neck got burned on the stairwell."
"That was so heroic of you," Kate said, proud of her husband's selfless bravery.

"You saved that little girl's life. Her mother will never forget you."

"I still get a Christmas card from the family every year." Tim smiled.

When they got back to their rooms after supper, Tim changed into his pajama bottoms and Kate into her new, black negligee. They packed their backpacks for tomorrow's hike, setting out their hiking shoes and socks. Before they went to bed, while Kate was still fussing in her backpack, Tim thought he'd call the local airlines about the flight to Molokai on Friday. He got a recording that said Thursday's flight to Molokai was the only one to and from the island this week. The plane departed at eight a.m. and returned at five p.m. He followed the prompt on the recording to be sure that their names were on the flight plan. How could I have missed that there is only one flight to Molokai each week—and on Thursdays? he ruminated. He knew he was in trouble with Kate; she had her heart set on going to the shrine. How can I tell her about the conflict between Haleakala and Molokai? he thought. It's too late to switch the reservations. He knew it was one or the other. He laid in bed dreading how to explain his mistake to Kate, as she cuddled next to him in the dark.

"Thanks for taking care of all the arrangements for our honeymoon, Tim," Kate whis- pered. "I was afraid at first, but I really enjoyed the snorkeling this afternoon. Things are going so well." She patted his strong chest.

"About that, babe," he said softly, then paused.

"About what?" Kate asked, snuggling beside him.

"I messed up," Tim said and kissed her head.

"I don't know how I did it, but I double-booked us tomorrow. There's only one flight to Molokai each week and it's on Thursdays, the same day I scheduled us for the hike up Haleakala."

"But you said we were going to Molokai on Friday," Kate said and raised her head.

"I know," Tim said, "but somehow I got the days mixed up. I forgot about the lone flight to the island on Thursdays. I guess I was so excited about the volcano that I didn't pay attention to the shrine's schedule. I just assumed that there would be a flight on Friday. I'm sorry."

"You knew the pilgrimage was so important to me," Kate said and began to tear up.

"How could you forget?" She turned away from him and began to sob.

Tim felt terrible about bringing his wife to tears on their honeymoon. He knew what he had to do. "We can still go to Molokai tomorrow. We're already packed and I checked our reservations on the plane. We're good to go." But his reassurance sounded hollow in the dark. Kate was still brooding with her back to Tim, the hurt unable to be wiped away with her tears. She knew her husband had never been enthusiastic about the pilgrimage to the shrine; not like he was about the hike up the volcano. And now it was evident; the damage was done.

"Babe," Tim said into the darkness. "I'm sorry. We'll go to Molokai, tomorrow; forget Haleakala," he said, sacrificing his only opportunity to scale the volcano and peer into the crater.

"Okay," she whispered between sniffles, but did not turn to hug her husband as they fell asleep.

When they awoke with the sunrise, Kate was unusually quiet. Tim sensed that she was giving him the cold shoulder, so he tried to engage her in some small talk about breakfast and the morning's flight, but she only grumbled in response and went into the bathroom.

"Oh, boy," Tim said under his breath, thinking that the short flight to Molokai Island might feel longer than the plane ride to Hawaii. "How could I have made such a stupid mistake?" he muttered, still feeling guilty that his thoughtlessness had caused Kate to cry.

Honeymoon

When she came out of the bathroom, she was still sullen. With the later departure, Kate took her time at the vanity, applying her makeup, brushing her hair, primping before the mirror. After Tim showered, they had some coffee and the sweet pastries that room service had delivered. They ate in relative silence compared to the rest of their honeymoon meals.

Kate was still sulking from Tim's oversight, upset that her husband could have forgotten something that he knew was so important to her.

In the lobby, Tim asked the concierge to call a cab for their drive to the airport.

"I'm glad we're wearing our hiking boots," Tim said once they entered the cab. "There's a couple dozen switchbacks as we hike down the hillside to the shrine."

"Yes, I know," Kate said curtly, having anticipated the arduous pilgrimage for months.

At the airport, the couple boarded the small propeller plane with their backpacks in tow.

They were the only ones booked for the short flight to Molokai Island, not the most popular destination for vacationers or honeymooners.

Molokai

"Well, on your way down the pali," the native pilot continued his tourist spiel. "Don't be surprised if you come across some feral pigs and goats. They're left-over from when the village was populated."

Kate asked the pilot who was left at the settlement.

"The nuns run the place, now," he said. "You'll see some of the thatched roofs over the flimsy huts, the cemetery, St. Philomena Church–they have a bookstore, too. But there haven't been many lepers since after Dr. Hansen found the cure around World War II."

"That's why they call it Hansen's Disease," Kate said for Tim's benefit, exhibiting her medical knowledge.

"I'm a kanaka," the pilot said. "I know it's not politically correct, but we still call it leprosy."

As the plane touched down and taxied to a stop on the thin airstrip at Kalawuao, the small community that lived on the plateau of the desolate island, the pilot offered some final instructions. "It'll take you about an hour, or so, to hike down the pali—you're young," he said.

"But, allow yourselves a few hours to hike back up. It's pretty steep and you'll want to rest along the way. I'll be here waiting for you at five p.m. sharp."

He helped the newlyweds step out of the plane and secure their backpacks. As they walked toward the van that was waiting for them, Tim turned around to say farewell to their pilot.

"We'll see you at five, Gus," Tim said, as much to reassure himself that they would be leaving Molokai at the end of the day as to confirm their flight plans with the pilot.

The short ride to the beginning of the pali trail took only a few minutes. Tim and Kate had just enough time to introduce themselves and secure the van for their return.

"I don't take many honeymooners to visit Kalawao," the driver, another kanaka, said. "Mostly pilgrims: nuns, priests, college kids—religious types."

Once out of the van, Tim and Kate walked toward the sign indicating the trail to Kalawao Village at the Kalaupapa National Park.

Peering over the five-hundred foot sheer cliff, Kate reached for Tim's hand before they began their trek.

"Thanks, Tim, for getting me here," she said, with the first tone of conciliation in her voice since last night.

"We almost didn't make it," Tim said, responding to her gentle demeanor. "We're here, now, babe. C'mon."

They proceeded tentatively along the narrow path. The trail wound back and forth along the steep pali, with a couple dozen switchbacks to enable hikers, and donkeys in the old days, to negotiate the steep cliff. Tim and Kate cautiously made their way past the patches of green shrubbery and occasional outgrowths of colorful wild flowers. Tim took the lead surveying the path ahead of them for rocks, roots, or depressions, that might cause Kate to stumble.

"Watch your step, honey," Tim said, kicking a small rock into the brush.

After several minutes, they fell into a steady, careful pace that enabled them to pause and touch hands during their hike toward the former leper colony.

"Look, there, Tim." Kate pointed to a delicate waterfall that descended from the path several feet ahead of them.

"Watch your step," Tim cautioned Kate. "It's a little muddy up here." He held her hand as they stepped through the puddle on the trail. "We're getting good use outta these boots."

As they continued, the couple instinctively grew more quiet, as if they sensed that they were nearing a sacred place. Kate noticed a little rockpile around a small crucifix in the shrubbery. She prayed a silent 'Our Father' in thanksgiving for their making it to another switchback on the trail, which put them better than two-thirds of the way down the pali. She noticed the air temperature seemed to get cooler the further they descended.

Tim heard a rustling in the shrubbery. "Maybe it's some of those feral animals," he said to Kate. "There's no snakes. Years ago, they imported mongoose from Europe to eradicate the native serpents," he explained, trying to impress his wife that he had done some reading about Molokai in the weeks before their honeymoon.

"Is it starting to rain?" Kate asked and held out her hands, palms up, to feel the water droplets. Tim mimicked his wife's gesture, then noticed that the droplets were being swept up from below by the strong, surf winds. "That's not rain, Kate; it's the spray from the wind and waves swirling up the pali."

"This far up?" she said incredulously.

"Yeah," Tim said, recalling what he had read about the ocean spray misting more than a hundred feet high along the face of the cliff. "Be careful. The trail might be a little slick." Hand-in-hand, the newlyweds walked cautiously toward the end of the trail, where the path seemed to widen. As they got closer to the beach, they could hear the splashing of the rough waves crashing against the big boulders along the shore. They stepped over some driftwood and rocks scattered on the beach until they finally found their footing in the sand. Dozens of small, yellow crabs scurried past them in the shallow stream of water that trickled on the surface of the sand. Kate tried to smooth her hair, but the strong, surf winds made it unmanageable.

Walking toward the cross atop the church steeple in the middle of the settlement a few hundred yards away, Kate was excited about completing the preliminary challenge of their pilgrimage.

"So, how did that pali form?" Kate asked Tim, consciously prompting him to expound on his geological knowledge of the Hawaiian Islands. "Such a sheer drop to the beach." "The volcano just slid into the ocean tens of thousands of years ago." Tim was pleased to have the opportunity to display his knowledge for the benefit of his wife.

"I'm sorry you won't get to climb Haleakala," Kate said softly.

"That's alright," Tim said. "I know you had your heart set on making this pilgrimage. I'm glad we're here." Though he was less than thrilled to be making a pilgrimage to a former leper colony on their honeymoon.

They walked in the balmy air past the cemetery to the chapel. St. Philomena's served for generations as the spiritual refuge for the leprous kanakas. Inside, Kate knelt before the tabernacle to offer her thanksgiving prayer to God for their safe arrival. Beside her, in the pew, Tim looked around at the simple appointments in the church; he was not accustomed to making weekday visits to the Blessed Sacrament. After a few minutes, they left the chapel to go to the visitor's center and bookstore.

In the quaint visitor's center of the shrine, they were met by a smiling Franciscan sister in her brown habit greeting them from behind the counter of the little bookstore, where she was arranging some religious items in the glass case.

"Good morning," she said and came out from behind the counter. "It's a beautiful day today."

"Good morning, Sister," Kate said, recognizing the familiar habit worn by the sisters at Syracuse. "We're from Syracuse, too. We're on our honeymoon."

Tim was happy to let Kate do the talking for both of them.

"Oh, that's wonderful," the sister said, reaching out to clasp Kate's hand. "We don't see any honeymooners."

"I just had to see the mission where Mother Marianne served the people with Fr. Damien," Kate said excitedly. "I'm a nurse—she inspired my vocation. This is my husband, Tim," she said. "I'm Kate."

"I'm Sister Stephanie," the friendly nun said. "Sister Clair will be joining me shortly. We run the shrine for the few visitors we get each week. Are you going to be on the islands for a few more days?"

"No," Tim answered. "We're leaving on Saturday. Tomorrow's our last day."

"That's why we hiked down the pali. I had to see the shrine," Kate said. "I want to pick up some things for my family. My mom volunteers at the motherhouse in Syracuse." "There's an updated biography of Mother's life," Sister Stephanie said and moved to the book display. "Since she's been canonized more people are interested in learning about her.

And then, when they moved her body back to our motherhouse in Syracuse, they can't keep them on the book shelves." Sister picked up one of the books and handed it to Kate. "We've gained a few novices, too."

Tim started looking around the bookstore for something that might interest him. "Thank you, Sister," Kate said. "Do you have a biography about Fr. Damien, too?" "Of course." Sister Stephanie moved to another display nearby and handed St. Damien's biography to Kate.

"It's for my husband," she whispered as she leaned closer to the nun. "I'm hoping he finds it inspiring."

Kate set the books on the countertop and began looking at the rosaries in the display case; she had a mind to buy them for her parents and her sisters.

"Those are made from koa, a native hardwood," Sister Stephanie said as she moved behind the counter and directed Kate to the dark, wood rosaries.

"Give me five pairs of those, Sister," Kate said, indicating the koa rosaries. "Better make it six—one for me, too."

Sister Stephanie placed the six pairs of rosary beads in individual boxes and put them in a gift bag for Kate.

"Hey, you better add this to your shopping spree," Tim said, placing a blue ballcap with the image of St. Philomena Church and the words 'Molokai-Hawaii' embossed in white with green trim, on the counter next to Kate's books and rosaries. "This will prove to the guys at the firehouse that I made a pilgrimage, too," he said, but he was actually more concerned that his souvenir would be considered 'acceptable' by his peers. He handed the nun their credit card.

Placing their items in their backpacks, Kate and Tim said 'good-bye' to the cordial nun and then turned toward the door.

"Do you have enough bottled water for the hike up the pali?" Sister Stephanie asked. "It's hot in the afternoon and you'll need to stay hydrated."

"Thanks," Kate said as they passed the cases of water near the door. "But we're okay, Sister. That's why these backpacks are so heavy."

Outside, Tim put his cap on as they surveyed the bleak grounds around the bookstore, the chapel, and the convent.

"Not much to see," Tim said as they approached the cemetery.

"Look at those trees," Kate said and pointed to the row of tall trees that were partially bent over, behind the rickety buildings.

"They planted them as windbreakers," Tim said, "to protect the people from the powerful winds off the ocean."

"You can see why they chose to isolate the lepers here, away from everything and everyone," Kate said.

"You gotta tip your hat to the priests and nuns who came here to help them," Tim said.

"That's why they're saints," Kate said. "The Church calls it heroic virtue." She stopped at a bench to retrieve a bottle of water from her backpack.

"Good idea," Tim said.

They both had long drinks of water as the late morning sun rose high and hot in the bright, blue sky.

Continuing to walk along the perimeter of the cemetery, they came to the stone monuments where Fr. Damien was buried and where St. Marianne's body was exhumed a few years ago to be returned to the motherhouse in New York.

Kate paused for a moment to pray. Tim took his cap off and silently prayed, too, though his was more a lament about the suffering of the lepers than a petition to heaven.

"Well, what'ya think, honey?" Tim said looking at his watch. "It's noon. I think we should be making our way back up the pali."

"Let's have something to eat first," Kate said. "There's a bench over there. I packed some nuts, dried fruit, and protein bars. And we have plenty of water."

"I'm hungry, too," Tim said as they sat on the bench facing the ocean, a soothing breeze cooling their faces. "It's kinda like a picnic."

They laughed together at their impromptu, rustic lunch at the edge of the cemetery. It was another of those quiet, still moments during their honeymoon when they paused from activity and simply enjoyed each other's company and their spouse's tender words of affection. Nearly an hour passed before they rose to begin the challenging hike back up the pali. Leaving the shrine site refreshed and eager to climb, Kate and Tim plodded their way along the beach, their boots digging into the sand.

"You can feel the afternoon sun," Tim said, tugging at the brim of his shrine ballcap. "You should've got a hat, too, Kate."

"My hair's enough to protect my head," she said. "And we'll be on the pali in a few minutes, anyhow."

They walked along the beach, hand in hand, toward the beginning of the path.

"Look up there, Tim," Kate said as she released her hand to point to a large white bird seemingly hovering on the currents of the wind above the thrashing ocean waters.

"That wingspan could be almost ten feet," Tim said. "There's a lot of exotic birds on the islands, but I didn't know there was anything that big."

"Look how long his tail is," Kate said. "I wonder what it's called. We'll have to ask the pilot when we get back on the plane."

They stopped to admire the large, white bird as it winged its way in the bright, blue sky beyond their sight.

Tim steadied Kate when the buffeting winds threw her off balance.

"Well, here we are," Tim said. "You ready?"

"I think so," Kate said, a little daunted, as they took their first steps up the pali trail.

They established a steady pace for the first several switchbacks until Kate paused for a drink of water.

"You can feel the sun," she said, wiping her brow with the back of her free hand, then taking a long drink with the other tilting the water bottle.

"My shirt's already soaked," Tim said and took a few swallows of water.

The couple renewed their trek as the trail became a little steeper. They weren't talking much, preserving their wind for the climb.

After a few more switchbacks, they paused again to hydrate.

"That nun was right," Tim said. "The afternoon sun is intense."

The brush along the trail was mostly low growing with an occasional taller, thin tree that shaded the pilgrims momentarily. After a few more switchbacks, Kate stopped to rest under a sparse tree. She sat on a rock that had some illegible writing scrawled on it; probably the names and dates of previous pilgrims. Tim stood a little ways away, gulping his water and wiping the sweat from his face. They took their backpacks off and rested for about fifteen minutes to get their second wind and replenish themselves with more water.

Beginning anew, Tim felt his calves tightening with the steeper grade. Kate felt the weight of her backpack, the straps irritating her shoulders. The sunlight had already dried up most of the wet spots on the trail; the random patches of wild flowers were the only respite for their tired eyes.

They walked with purpose, now, realizing they were more than halfway up the pali trail. After another half-an-hour, Kate found another shady spot and sat down on a broken tree limb to rest and drink. Tim was ahead of her a few yards on the turn of another switchback, so he stopped to keep her in sight.

Kate heard a bleating sound and then saw a kid goat emerge from the brush. He came right toward her and pressed his head against her blue jeans. She reached down and smoothed her hand along his rough, gray coat. He was panting and rested against her leg, seemingly lost.

"Where's your mother, baby?" she whispered to the feral animal and continued to stroke his back.

Meanwhile, Tim was observing the unfolding drama from a short distance away. Kate poured some water into her cupped hand and placed it near the mouth of the little goat. He lapped up the water greedily. She did it a few more times until the kid seemed to have his fill. Then his head perked up and Kate heard the bleating of another goat.

Immediately, the kid bounded off toward the recognizable sound, probably, of his mother's call.

"Go, go," Kate whispered after the kid as it disappeared into the brush.

Tim walked over to Kate and helped her up. "Looks like you saved another lost soul," he said. He saw a tear on her cheek and wiped it off.

"Did you see him go running when he heard her call?" she said.

"I saw the whole thing," he said. "You're amazing, babe."

After he helped her secure her backpack, they continued along the path. It would take another hour, or so, for them to complete the strenuous hike up the pali. Before they reached the top, Tim's right calf cramped and he had to stop and stretch his leg until the knot subsided.

Kate tried to ease the tightness in the muscle with a gentle massage through his jeans.

"Drink some more water," she directed her patient. They were both soaked with sweat. When they finally completed the hike a little before five o'clock, they found their driver waiting for them near the park sign.

Flopping into the van, they were happy to rest on the cushioned seats for the short ride to the airport. Tim's calf was still a little sore.

"Well," their driver said. "Was it worth it?"

"Yes," Kate said. "A little desolate. The sister we met at the bookstore was very friendly."

"I see you got a souvenir," the driver said, alluding to Tim's ball cap.

"It helped for the hike up the pali," Tim said. "It was hot."

"It's in the mid-nineties, today," their driver said and pulled up to the airport.

"There's Gus on the air strip waiting for you."

Tim paid the cabby and gave him a generous tip. He carried Kate's backpack to the plane to relieve the pressure on her shoulders from the straps. The pilot helped them board.

Once they were settled in the plane, Gus reminded them to fasten their seat belts. Before they knew it, they were airborne and on their way to Maui.

They kissed in the back seat, despite their sweaty faces—a kind of seal for the completion of the pilgrimage.

"Well," the pilot said. "What do you think?"

"It was something," Tim said; Kate was already dozing against him. "That hike up the pali in the afternoon sun took it out of us."

"Not much to see, hunh," the pilot said.

"We saw a huge, white bird flying above the shore," Tim said. "It's wingspan could've been ten feet wide; it had real long tail feathers. Do you know what it's called?"

Something that big could only be the koae kea," he said. "They normally nest in Maui, on the ledges inside the craters. You seldom see them on Molokai. They're better known as the white-tailed tropic bird. They spend most of their life at sea hunting for food."

"I never knew there was anything that big on the islands," Tim said.

"The kanaka would say it was a good omen for your marriage," the pilot offered. "We're still a little superstitious under our religion," he chuckled.

As the plane landed at the Maui airport, Kate woke up.

"Kate," Tim said softly. "That bird is called koae kea. He said you see them more around Maui, nesting in the craters."

"Koae kea," Kate repeated the name.

"He said the locals would say our seeing one around Molokai was a good omen for our future," Tim said and gently touched her hand.

"I hope so," Kate said.

During the cab ride from the airport to their hotel, the couple discussed what they wanted to do: eat or sleep.

"We can always order room service after our nap," Kate said.

"I'm more tired than hungry," Tim said. "My calf is still a little sore."

So, when they got to their suite, they took off their backpacks and hiking boots, and socks, undressed quickly and flopped down on the newly-made bed in their underwear, their tired feet atop the soft duvet at the bottom of the bed. Tim hung his shrine cap on the bedpost.

The coolness of the air conditioning helped them to fall asleep.

When they awoke a couple of hours later, it was already dark.

"I'm hungry," Tim said. "I need some meat after that birdseed we had for lunch."

"That 'birdseed' kept us alive, Mister," Kate said feigning annoyance at Tim's quip, though it was funny.

Kate called room service. "They have some pork from the luau they can send up with some sides," she said to Tim.

"Sounds great," he said.

"I told them in about half-an-hour so we have a chance to freshen up," Kate said.

With their order placed, they walked into their spacious bathroom. Removing their underwear, they looked at each other sheepishly. They had never showered together before.

"It is our honeymoon," Tim said as he turned on the water in the marble shower." It'll save time."

"Not too hot," Kate said.

Tim adjusted the water temperature just right. He took her hand and helped her step into the shower. The warm water felt good on their sore bodies, especially their backs and legs. They luxuriated for half of an hour in the soapy shower, though they were both hungry after the day's excursion.

They donned the white hotel bath robes and slippers as they dried their hair in the bathroom.

At the knock on the door, Tim went to welcome room service with their cart of supper.

When he opened the door, the savory aroma of the roasted pork wafted into the suite. Tim retrieved some bills for the tip from his jeans laying on the divan. When the server left, Kate came out of the bathroom and joined Tim at the small table in their dining area.

Their dinner consisted of strips of succulent kalua pig cooked in an underground oven or imu, mashed sweet potatoes, and some spicy, marinated kimchi cabbage. Kate gracefully served generous portions on their plates, giving Tim some extra pieces of the roasted pork.

From the room's mini refrigerator, Tim got a small bottle of chardonnay for Kate and a wine glass from the nearby cupboard. He also brought a couple of bottles of a local beer to the table for himself with a tall glass. The hungry couple ate voraciously, their appetites stimulated by the grueling afternoon hike up the pali. Kate gave Tim more of the delicious pork before he even asked for it. They both enjoyed second helpings of the sweet potatoes and tasty cabbage. The pineapple, passion fruit, and sweet lychee were the perfect dessert to cleanse their palates. Lingering at the table after their meal, they clinked glasses in a toast Tim offered to his beautiful bride whose determined dream had gotten them to Hawaii.

With their hunger sated and the alcohol soothing their minds, they took off their hotel robes and slipped their tired bodies into bed for a deep, deserved sleep.

While she slept, Kate dreamt about her wedding at St. Joseph's. Walking down the center aisle of the Church in her beautiful wedding gown, she felt a rush of wind coming from behind her, unfurling her long veil into the air, and then hearing the flapping of the wings of the white koae kea as it flew before her toward the sanctuary. In her dream, the seabird's wings extended over the congregation, enveloping the people in a 'swoosh' of wind that, somehow, harmonized with the mellifluous wedding march emanating from the organ. Kate stirred momentarily but did not awaken from her deep sleep.

Meanwhile, beside her, Tim's memory conjured the rescue of the little girl from the housefire in a dream of him flying down the blazing staircase and out of the front door onto the lawn where his colleague doused him with a stream of water from the fire hose, causing smoke to rise from his long coat, the mother's 'Thank you's' resounding all around them, louder than the crackling fire, as she embraced her daughter. Tim awoke, momentarily, and instinctively touched the scar on his neck and scalp. Then, he fell back to sleep, exhausted.

They slept past sunrise, past breakfast, and finally awoke about eleven o'clock. They were slow to get out of bed, and, when they did, they both moaned with soreness. The climb up the pali had challenged their young, healthy bodies, especially Tim's back and Kate's feet. They remained lying down for a few minutes before they dared to roll out of bed. Tim was first to slowly swing his legs out of the bed and plop his feet down.

"Coffee," he mumbled. "Coffee."

Kate turned her lithe frame to get out of bed, her sore feet easing into the plush carpet.

"I thought we were in better shape," she said.

"I'm stiff all over," Tim said as he slowly twisted his torso to loosen his back.

"My feet hurt," Kate said as she tried to get up.

"That's the price we pay for doing something good," Tim said, alluding to their pilgrimage.

"Don't make me laugh," she said, her arms pressing against her ribs. Then she put on her robe.

"Can you order a big pot of coffee and some breakfast rolls, honey," Tim said, still sitting on the side of the bed.

"A big pot for sure," Kate said. "Do you want any fruit?"

"Coffee," Tim said. "I just need some coffee."

Kate made her way to the phone and ordered the coffee, rolls, and fruit. "Put your robe on, Tim," she said.

He groaned as he stretched his arms through the sleeves of his robe.

They had their Kona coffee and sweet rolls in the quiet of their gracious suite on this last day of their honeymoon. They nibbled on the fruit. Neither of them were in a hurry to get ready nor to start packing their suitcases. They both felt a little nostalgic as they realized their blissful days in Hawaii were coming to an end. So, they climbed back into bed for awhile, relishing the peace of their noon rest, their young bodies less sore and more supple, now.

"You're something, babe," Tim said and touched her hand.

"You know, before I met you," Kate said. "I never liked it when guys called their girlfriends babe or honey, or some other pet name. But when you do it, it thrills me because I know how you mean it. You mean that you would love and protect me with your very life because I'm yours. Like you did that little girl." She squeezed his hand.

They turned toward each other in their hotel robes and kissed.

Eventually, they would rise and wash, pack their suitcases, and smooth over any tensions that had arisen in the past week, like Tim's scheduling oversight. They dressed in their best vacation outfits: Kate in a breezy, floral dress; Tim in his colorful Hawaiian shirt and khakis. At about six o'clock they went downstairs for a last meal in the elegant hotel dining room. Somehow, the maitre d' knew it was their final night and sent a bottle of champagne to their table. Their pretty Polynesian waitress could not have been more solicitous, smiling everytime she approached them.

After the romantic supper, Tim and Kate returned to their honeymoon suite for a good night's rest. Their flight left early the next morning for Oahu and, then, from there, they would take the long flight to the mainland.

They checked their luggage and souvenirs, securing their tickets, his wallet, her purse, and a few other essentials. While Tim became engrossed reading about the heroic life of Fr. Damien de Veuster, who eventually died like the lepers he served, his skin pockmarked with sores and scars, Kate was in the bathroom preparing herself for the final night of their honeymoon in Hawaii. She emerged from the bathroom in her lacy, black negligee, perfumed and sauntering past her husband, whose eyes were buried in his book. Catching a scent of her tropical fragrance, he looked up and saw his beautiful wife sashay by him. He set the book down and playfully chased her around the suite until she caught him. The wayfarers spent the last night of their honeymoon communing in each other's arms, as God intended.

Printed in the USA
CPSIA information can be obtained
at www.ICGtesting.com
CBHW070737270424
7563CB00004B/9

9 781950 607167